A Novelette of **ANCIENT ASSYRIA** *in the Days of Jonah*

LAMASSU
FALLING

ARTURO R. ORTIZ

LUCIDBOOKS

Lamassu Falling

A Novelette of Ancient Assyria in the Days of Jonah

Copyright © 2024 by Arturo Ortiz

Published by Lucid Books in Houston, TX

www.LucidBooks.com

ISBN: 978-1-63296-652-0

eISBN: 978-1-63296-653-7

Special Sales: Most Lucid Books titles are available in special quantity discounts. Custom imprinting or excerpting can also be done to fit special needs. Contact Lucid Books at Info@LucidBooks.com

TABLE OF CONTENTS

Acknowledgment   v

Chapter 1: Tribulation Begins   1

Chapter 2: Portent in the Heavens   9

Chapter 3: War and Rumors of War   19

Chapter 4: Plagues in the Land   25

Chapter 5: An Interrupted Journey   37

Chapter 6: They Are Coming for the Children   53

Chapter 7: Peace in the Land   77

ACKNOWLEDGMENT

I am grateful to Ivonne Ileana Rodriguez for insightful comments she provided during the writing of this novelette.

CHAPTER 1
TRIBULATION BEGINS

It is the year of Ninip-Mukin-Nisi in the chronicles of the kings of Assyria. Assyria rules the world with an iron fist. King Ashurdan rules Assyria. The year begins like any other. Unknown to the people of Assyria, it is destined to become a year like no other.

A rider on a fast horse approaches the east gate of the citadel of Nimrud, home of the king's palace, a day's ride south of the great city of Nineveh along the River Tigris. Assyrian soldiers stand guard at the gate keeping close watch over all who seek entry into the citadel. When the rider reaches the gate, a soldier says, "Stop! All who seek entry into the king's citadel must declare their name and purpose of visit."

The rider replies, "I am Albazi, servant of the great and honorable King Ashurdan. I bring a message of utmost importance to the king and his great ones."

The soldier commands Albazi to wait while he sends a messenger to the guards of the northwest palace complex. After a minimal delay, he receives word that Albazi is to be admitted to the king's throne room. He orders the gate be opened, and he commands Albazi to pass through the gate. Mounted soldiers meet Albazi to escort him to the northwest palace complex.

The entourage proceeds from the gate along a short road and arrives at a spot where the road separates into three branches, each leading to a different sector of the citadel. The entourage continues along the middle branch, which leads to the main entrance of the northwest palace complex. The men dismount at the entrance and continue on foot. They cross a large open space; pass through a covered corridor; cross a second, smaller open space; pass through another covered corridor; and arrive at the outer courtyard of the northwest palace complex. The men enter the outer courtyard, veer to the left, and arrive at the immense gate of the Great Northern Courtyard. They pass through the gate and veer to the left toward the main building of the northwest palace complex. There, they behold two very tall arched portals, both guarded by pairs of enormous lamassus facing outward toward the Great Northern Courtyard.

A lamassu is a statue of a winged bull with five legs and a crowned human male head. At least four legs are visible regardless of the viewer's perspective. The face has an elaborately braided beard and displays an imposing countenance. Lamassus are symbols of the power and might of Assyria. They always appear in pairs, always facing outward from the entrance to a building or grand hall. Assyrians believe that lamassus provide magical protection from evil spirits.

The entourage approaches the portal on the right, which has huge double doors that open directly into the royal throne room. Standing guard at the portal are two robust bearded palace servants clad in fine robes with sashes. The servants open the double doors and let the entourage through.

The throne room is grand and majestic, rising high above the palace complex. The walls are painted in dazzling blue, and are richly decorated with artwork, including paintings and gypsum reliefs. The artwork displays the military might of Assyria, the authority of the king, and some hunting scenes. Most of the artwork is from the days of the mighty and ruthless conquering king Ashurnasirpal, who trampled the surrounding nations more than a hundred years ago. The entourage veers to the left and proceeds toward the royal throne at the far end of the room, passing tall blazing lampstands along the way. They pass a bed of hot coals that keeps the room warm and then stop right in front of the royal throne. Behind the throne are images of sacred trees tended by powerful winged creatures known as *apkallu*. The apkallu are lesser gods of Assyria; some are depicted with human heads and others with the heads of eagles. To the right is the entrance to a grand hall guarded by another pair of imposing lamassus.

Ashurdan, strong king, king of Assyria, king of the world, king of the four quarters, is seated on the throne. He is arrayed in a royal blue, fringed robe and a fringed scarlet sash. In keeping with his kingly stature, he is wearing royal jewelry, fine sandals, and the distinctive conical hat of Assyrian kings with its pair of long tassels. He holds a mace in his right hand, symbolizing the authority vested in him as vice-regent of Assyria's supreme god. His beard is braided. Several great ones dressed in fine regalia stand next to the throne along with eunuchs, aides, and royal guards.

The eunuchs are wise and educated advisors to the king. Their appearance is effeminate. They are dressed in fine robes with colorful fringed sashes; their hair is long, but they have no beards. One eunuch stands right beside the seated king, holding a sickle in one hand. It is his solemn duty to use his sickle to fight off any demons that attack the king. That eunuch is one of an elite corps of highly trusted servants who are allowed to bear arms near the king. They guard the king day and night.

Albazi bows before the king. "Rise and speak, Albazi," said Ashurdan.

Albazi rises and says, "Great and honorable king, I bring a message of the utmost importance. Pestilence is spreading quickly throughout the land. People are perishing in large numbers. Horses, donkeys, cattle, and goats are dying. Mountains of dead are rising in several cities. The loss of beasts of burden is disrupting harvests and transportation chains, and we can expect shortages of grain and meat. An outbreak of famine may be imminent, and in time, we might have food riots. Moreover, poverty spreads throughout the land as husbands perish and their wives become poor widows. Many children are orphans because both parents have died. Conditions are particularly bad in the cities of Ashur, Arbaha, and Gozan."

Ashurdan is very concerned. There has not been an outbreak of plague in Assyria in a very long time. He thinks this may become a year like no other in memory. He is right. And more bad news is coming.

Ashurdan seeks counsel from his great ones. One says, "We should immediately start buying grain from Egypt. Over a thousand years ago, there was famine throughout the entire world, but Egypt's storehouses had abundant supplies of grain. It is said that in those days, Pharaoh commanded the filling of storehouses with surplus grain during plentiful years in preparation for lean years. Let us turn westward to Egypt and send envoys to purchase grain from Pharaoh. We have sufficient gold and silver to pay for large purchases of grain."

Another great one says, "While we turn westward to Egypt for grain, we should turn eastward to Persia for meat. Let us send envoys to Persia to buy cattle."

Another great one says, "Babylon is rich in food and other resources. Let us turn southward to Babylon and send envoys to purchase food. We may also need to rely more on fish from our rivers and lakes to feed the people."

"Your counsels are wise," said Ashurdan. "I will dispatch envoys to Egypt, Persia, and Babylon to buy food. Moreover, I will dispatch surgeons to the suffering cities to treat the sick, and I will dispatch agricultural workers to the suffering farmlands to assist with harvests and help care for sick animals. I will command the stewards of storehouses to give a full tally of our grain supplies. Meanwhile, prepare an emergency plan for distribution of rations. We will get through this crisis."

He says to his aide, "Summon the high priests of the great gods. We need major increases in supplication and sacrifices to the gods."

𒅓 𒂊𒀉 𒅓𒌋

It is a day like any other in the main square of the great city of Nineveh. People are going about their usual business. Merchants are selling and customers are buying. The pious are burning incense to the great gods at small altars throughout the square. The taverns and brothels have their usual patrons. The local slave market is auctioning slaves.

Rabbu and Tamraz are going about their usual business in the square. Both served in the king's army and proved themselves brave and fierce in combat. Rabbu was known as the "mighty one," and many of Assyria's foes fell by a stroke of Rabbu's sword. Tamraz was known as the "strong dog." He was the best spearman in the Assyrian army. He never missed. With a single throw of a spear, he would impale three enemy soldiers like balls of meat on a skewer. When Rabbu and Tamraz served together in the war against the Hittites in the north country, they established a lasting friendship.

After serving in the army, Rabbu became a merchant. He owns and runs a very successful shop in the city square. Rabbu is handsome. Many young maidens desire him, but he has eyes for only one woman, Adorina, the daughter of Nabukinuzur, a nobleman and one of the ruling great ones of Nineveh. Much as he longed for Adorina, Rabbu could not have her, since he is a commoner, and Adorina is of noble birth.

Adorina is one of the fairest maidens in the land. She has an exquisite figure. Her long, wavy tresses gleam in the sunlight like polished chestnut. They are parted in the middle so that half of her hair falls in front of her right shoulder and half behind her left shoulder. Her face is like fine porcelain marked by rosy cheeks and luscious lips. Her enchanting eyes sparkle like gemstones, and a light shade of azure eye shadow brightens them even more. Her arms are milky white. Heads turn whenever Adorina walks into a room. She has many suitors of noble birth, but her heart is set on a commoner called Rabbu. Much as she longed for Rabbu, Adorina could not have him, since she is of noble birth, and Rabbu is a commoner.

After serving in the army, Tamraz became a stonecutter. He is a big man with a rugged appearance, and strong as a bull. When people see him, they think of Gilgamesh, the mighty hero of the immortal epic that bears that name. Tamraz is popular with the young maidens of Nineveh, as many of them want a strong man like Tamraz for a husband, but Tamraz would not settle for just one woman. He would enter a tavern alone and come out later with at least three women. Two would be in his arms, and one would be sitting on his shoulders. Sometimes, he indulges in too much drink and gets into brawls. He easily wrestles to the ground any man who challenges him. Sometimes he would wrestle and subdue three challengers at the same time and arise unscathed by the scuffle. They say it is better to be pounded by a battering ram than to be struck by Tamraz's fists. Some brawlers found that out the hard way.

Adorina is shopping at the square. She is wearing a fine lavender linen dress accented with a fringed scarlet sash and fine sandals. Her accessories are worthy of a princess—a gold bracelet, gold ring, gold earrings, gold necklace, and a gold headband.

She visits Rabbu's shop. "Rabbu, come to my house again soon," she said with a smile. "I always enjoy playing the Royal Game of Ur with you."

"Not fair," said Rabbu. "You always win. You play the game too well."

"That is because you have not mastered the rules," said Adorina. "It is a game of strategy. You should know about strategy from your service in the army."

"Come now, Adorina," said Rabbu. "Officers learn strategy. I was just a regular foot soldier."

"Not so," said Adorina. "You were one of the most decorated soldiers in the army—you and your big friend, Tamraz. Remember, I was there cheering for both of you at the awards ceremony. Anyway, come over. I will serve you a delicious platter of fresh locust with tasty dipping sauce."

"You just convinced me," said Rabbu. "How about tonight?"

"Tonight it is, Rabbu," said Adorina. "Be sure and come with a healthy appetite." Then she went about her shopping. Rabbu gazed at her admiringly as she walked away. Whenever he sees Adorina, his heart pounds mightily, and he feels dizzy as if his head is spinning.

Tamraz was strolling nearby and heard the entire conversation between Adorina and Rabbu. He says, "Rabbu, so many fair women in the city, but you are set on Nabukinuzur's daughter."

Rabbu says, "Whenever I see Adorina, I am enchanted. She is so beautiful. Her eyes outshine the starry host. I get dizzy.

My head spins. My heart melts. I desire her for my bride more than anything in this world. And I know she likes me. But the authorities will never allow a commoner like me to marry a woman of noble birth."

"But there are so many pretty young maidens of common birth who admire you, Rabbu," said Tamraz. "Surely, you can find your bride among them."

"No, my friend," said Rabbu. "I have eyes only for Adorina."

"As for me, one woman can never be enough," said Tamraz. "I see myself as being generous to the maidens."

"Yes, I noticed that, Tamraz," said Rabbu. "Three, four, even five at a time. Will you ever settle for just one?"

"Look around and see all the pretty maidens," said Tamraz. "How can I settle for just one above the rest?"

CHAPTER 2

PORTENT IN THE HEAVENS

It is the year of Zadkiel in the chronicles of the kings of Assyria. Turmoil is engulfing the mighty nation. The worst of the pestilence has passed, but its economic impact lingers. The loss of farm animals has crippled Assyria's agriculture. As the nation's storehouses are emptying, shortages of grain, meat, and milk afflict the land. Famine begins to spread. The enormous loss of beasts of burden has crippled transportation throughout the land. It is with great difficulty that Assyria assembles the large caravans needed to bring enough food from Egypt, Persia, and Babylon. Unrest spreads throughout the land. Ashurdan receives reports of food riots in several major cities. He summons his great ones and says to them, "Surely, things will improve over time. The great gods will see us through." He is wrong.

One day, the high priest of Ashur, god of war, addresses Ashurdan. "Great and honorable king, it is the king's duty to command a military campaign each year to bring war booty to our nation. As you know, we need war booty to build temples, palaces, canals, and other public works. We must conquer foreign lands and bring back slaves, gold, silver, tin, copper, bronze, iron, and building materials. If we do not get more slaves and booty, our massive building projects cannot be finished. May I remind the king that many slaves perished during the pestilence. We can work our remaining slaves to death, but dead slaves do no work. Who will do the work if we have a shortage of slaves? What will the slaves work with if we have shortages of materials? With what money will we fund our building projects without gold and silver from conquered lands? May I also remind the king that it is your duty to the great gods to bring back treasures from conquered lands so we can fill our temples with spoils of war. What will become of our temples without more treasures? Great and honorable king, you must lead us to war at once. Choose a rich neighbor to invade so we may plunder him and impose tribute on him. The great gods will bless you if you do. They will curse you if you do not."

Ashurdan is troubled. He rises from his throne, paces about the room for a few moments, and says, "I find myself in a most difficult situation. Our economy is in ruin on account of the pestilence. To conduct a major military campaign, we will need to assemble a host of at least one hundred thousand men in arms, along with chariots and horses. Not possible. We can barely assemble caravans to buy desperately needed food from Egypt, Persia, and Babylon. A war of conquest at this time is out of the question. Even the great gods must concede as much."

"Great and honorable king, with what authority do you say what the great gods must concede?" asked the high priest. "That borders on blasphemy. Retract your words so the great gods might relent from punishing us."

"High priest," said Ashurdan, "sometimes I wonder how much of your pious chatter arises from truth and how much arises from superstition."

"Blasphemy!" shouted the high priest.

"No, it is reality," said Ashurdan. "Domestic challenges take precedence over expeditions to foreign lands. I have a nation to feed. Moreover, some of our unfriendly neighbors may want to exploit this time of weakness for Assyria. If we have a war, it will be one to repel invasion. The king and the army will remain in the land. I have spoken, and it will be as I have spoken. One more thing, high priest. Never again accuse me of blasphemy. Mind your tongue, or you may lose it someday. You are dismissed!"

Ashurdan summons his royal scribe and says to him, "Let it be recorded in the chronicles of the kings of Assyria that in this year of Zadkiel, the king remained in the land."

The year dragged on, and things did not improve. To the four quarters of the land, the confidence of the people was eroded. But that was only the beginning; more tribulation was coming.

𒀭 𒂍𒁉 𒀭𒌋

It is the year of Esdu-Sarabe in the chronicles of the kings of Assyria. In the month of Sivan, the people of the land see a rare event as they look up to the sky. The moon is crossing in front of the sun, and the brightness of day is being blotted out. Assyria is going through a major solar eclipse. There has not been a major solar eclipse over Assyria in a very long time. The people are frightened, for they know a major solar eclipse is a portent of calamities to come.

Astrologers in Nineveh are monitoring the eclipse. Slowly but surely, the moon occludes more of the sun until total darkness descends on the great city around midday. The sky is as black as the darkest night, and the stars shine through. The astrologers are filled with fear.

The chief astrologer speaks to his colleagues. "Do you understand the implications of this portent? It is written in our ancient sacred tablets that a major solar eclipse is a sign that tribulation is coming to our land. Indeed, we have been suffering tribulation these past three years. It is also written that the city that sees a total solar eclipse is doomed. Here at Nineveh, we see a total solar eclipse. Our great city is doomed. Woe to Nineveh!"

"What shall we do?" asked one of the astrologers.

"We must perform the ritual of the substitute king," replied the chief astrologer. "Send word to Hormuzd, the king's personal astrologer, at the citadel of Nimrud. Hormuzd will explain things to the king."

The next day, Hormuzd comes before the king to explain the meaning of the eclipse. "Great and honorable king, we hold to the astrological beliefs recorded in the ancient sacred Babylonian tablets containing the Enuma Anu Enlil. A major eclipse seen over our land is an omen that tribulation is coming to the land. The king will perish, and a worthless fellow will seize the throne. The land will be afflicted by wars, plagues, and earthquakes. But the city that sees a total solar eclipse is doomed to be wiped off the face of the earth. Our land saw a major solar eclipse, but the great city of Nineveh saw a total solar eclipse. Nineveh is destined to be wiped off the face of the earth. Woe to the great city of Nineveh!"

Ashurdan places his face in his hands and ponders the implications of Hormuzd's words. He raises his head and asks, "What must we do?"

Hormuzd replies, "We must perform a ritual that has not been performed in this land in a very long time. The king must be taken to a secret place where he can hide until the danger passes. A temporary substitute king and queen must be chosen. The real king will continue to issue government orders from the secret place while the substitute king and queen live in the king's palace. The substitute king will wear the king's royal garments and participate in the usual kingly rituals. After the danger passes, the substitute king and queen are to be sacrificed to the great gods. They must die as substitutionary sacrifices in the place of the real king. Then the real king returns to his throne to complete the ritual. Great and honorable king, you must authorize initiation of this ritual to save your own life. I suggest we also take actions to protect the inhabitants of the great city."

"How long must I remain in hiding, and who must be chosen to be substitute king and queen?" asked Ashurdan.

Hormuzd replies, "In the past, the king remained in hiding for about one hundred days. If the danger passes sooner, the king returns sooner. Regarding the choice of substitute king and queen, the custom is to select a common man and a common woman. They may be poor people, people of ill repute, even criminals. Since they are to be sacrificed in the end, it is wise to choose people who will not be missed when normal times return. Moreover, it is easy to get poor people to volunteer, since they know they will live in luxury with fine dining, clothing, and entertainment. A poor man who has no woman of his own is more likely to volunteer, especially knowing he will be given an attractive maiden as his substitute queen and wife."

Ashurdan asks, "If Nineveh is still standing after one hundred days, do we assume that the danger has passed and that I can return to my throne?"

Hormuzd replies, "Yes, if Nineveh is still standing after one hundred days, we may assume the danger has passed and you can return to your throne. However, tribulation may linger in the land for some time."

Ashurdan ponders Hormuzd's words. Then he says, "Find among the inhabitants of Nineveh suitable choices for substitute king and queen, preferably volunteers. Tell them of the good times they will enjoy, but also tell them how the times will end for them. Since they will be sacrificed in the end, choose not from the high and noble, but from those of lowly stature. Promise them they will live in the royal palace and dine in luxury with fine wine and merriment until the time they are to be sacrificed. So let it be done."

Hormuzd says, "We will do as you have commanded, great and honorable king. With your permission, I take leave of you now. I have much to do in very little time."

The national authorities dutifully implemented the ritual of the substitute king. Ashurdan was taken to a secret place in accordance with the ritual. A Ninevite knave called Barsawme was chosen as substitute king. Barsawme knew he must die at the end. Even so, he was glad to accept the assignment. He is a man of most humble means. But now, for at least a little while, he gets to live in the opulent northwest palace complex of Nimrud. He will dress each day in royal regalia and dine in luxury in the palace. Fine food and fine drink will be served to him each day, and he will enjoy entertainment and merriment each evening. An attractive young woman of most humble means, called Ghezalle, was given to Barsawme as his substitute queen. She too will delight in the opulence, luxury, fine dining, and entertainment of royal palace life, until the day Ashurdan returns from hiding. On that day, Barsawme and Ghezalle will be sent off to their eternal destinies.

𒀭 𒂍𒀲 𒀭𒌋

Barsawme is required to perform the king's ritual duties. One day, three royal priests arrive to instruct him regarding libations to be offered to the great gods.

The priests stand before the royal throne, and the first priest speaks. "Sire, we come to instruct you regarding the libations you must offer to the great gods."

Barsawme slouches on the throne, drunk and uninterested, holding a large wine goblet in his left hand and a large lamb chop in his right hand. After munching on the lamb chop and gulping down some wine, he belches loudly and obnoxiously.

Barsawme says, "Do not bother me with trivialities. I want more wine and more food! I want some pretty young maidens at my side. Go find my queen. Send in musicians and dancing girls. I want to be entertained!"

"But sire!" exclaimed the priest, "Our religion requires that you offer the libations. We are here to instruct you on your ritual duties."

"I am your substitute king!" exclaimed Barsawme. "I command you to obey me and please me. Send me more wine, food, pretty maidens, musicians, and dancers. I will enjoy to the fullest my one hundred days as substitute king. Go away and do not bother me with religious affairs or affairs of state." He takes another bite of his lamb chop, gulps down more wine, and belches again.

The priest rolls his eyes and says, "As you wish, sire. My fellow priests, let us take leave of our substitute king."

The priests leave the royal throne room. On their way out, they speak unflatteringly of Barsawme. "What do you think of our great and honorable substitute king?" asked the first priest in an undisguised sarcastic tone.

"That melonhead!" exclaimed the second priest. "He is a gluttonous fool, an oaf, a knave, and a drunkard."

"You are too generous to him," said the third priest. "He is a worthless pighead. He appears to be rather stupid. I suppose if they lock him up in a room with no food or water, he will die from stupidity before he dies from hunger or thirst." The three priests laughed.

"I can see why they chose him as substitute king to be sacrificed in the end," said the second priest. "Surely, our national authorities would not allow a good man to be wasted that way."

"I suppose you are right," said the first priest. "But now we have more important matters to attend to. Our nation is in turmoil. It is up to us to intercede with the great gods for the sake of our nation. We will just have to perform our duties without him."

Two soldiers overheard the priests. One soldier says, "You know what? If they give me a charming pretty lady for a wife, I might be willing to become the substitute king."

"Are you out of your mind?" asked the other soldier. "Do you not know that both of you will be sacrificed in the end? No woman is worth that."

"What about the pretty girl who serves drinks in the palace dining hall?" asked the soldier. "The one with long black hair? She might be worth it!"

"I know which girl you mean," said the other soldier. "All the unmarried men in the palace lust after her. Come to think of it, half of the married men want her too!" Both laughed and then went about their business.

𒈦 𒂗 𒈦𒌋

A few weeks later, the one hundred days expired. Nineveh still stands. Hormuzd announces to the royal court that it is time for the substitute king and queen to be given to the great gods and for Ashurdan to return to his throne. Barsawme hears Hormuzd's words, but he is too drunk to care.

The next day Barsawme and Ghezalle are led to the temple of the great god Nabu in Nimrud to be sacrificed. Both are dressed in fine regalia. They ride in an elaborately ornamented chariot pulled by royal stallions. The atmosphere is that of a carnival. The people watch and cheer, expecting better days. As usual, Barsawme is drunk, even as he rides to his death, still gulping wine from a large goblet in his left hand and munching on a large lamb chop in his right hand, belching along the way. Ghezalle is drunk too, but at least she waves to the crowds while Barsawme only stuffs himself.

The priests of Nabu watch the procession. The high priest says, "No great loss to our nation, those two."

Another priest says, "I hope the great gods are not too offended when they meet those two."

Yet another priest says, "I am more afraid the great gods might send them back to us."

"Be quiet," said the high priest. "Do not give them any ideas." At that, the priests laughed and went about their business.

The chariot carrying Barsawme and Ghezalle entered the temple precinct. Temple servants shut the gates behind the chariot. A little while later, Barsawme and Ghezalle departed to their eternal destinies.

CHAPTER 3

WAR AND RUMORS OF WAR

The people expected better days after the real king returned. Their expectations were dampened by the outbreak of a violent uprising in the major city of Ashur, south of Nineveh.

An aide approaches Ashurdan's throne. "Great and honorable king," he said, "we received reports of a revolt in the major city of Ashur. The city governor was overthrown, and a usurper made himself ruler of the city. Word has it that he promised to fix the food shortages in Ashur. He also promised that if the people follow him, he will protect them during the bad times foretold by the recent eclipse. Apparently, he has been building a following for some time. Great and honorable king, if this revolt is not quenched soon, the entire land may lapse into civil war."

Ashurdan rises from his throne and paces nervously about the room. Then he says, "Send word to the Nineveh garrison to march immediately to Nimrud. Prepare the Nimrud garrison for departure. When the Nineveh garrison arrives, we will add its strength to the Nimrud garrison and proceed south to Ashur as a combined force. We will suppress the revolt, seize the usurper and his lackeys, and impale them on stakes for all to see. Even so, we must also deliver food to the suffering people of Ashur."

𒀭 𒂍 𒀭𒀝

It is the year of Dabu-Bel in the chronicles of the kings of Assyria. The combined garrisons of Nineveh and Nimrud have been battling the rebels of Ashur for some time, but the revolt persists, with no end in sight. That is ominous news for Ashurdan. Usually, when Assyrian soldiers march off to war, they fall on the enemy with great slaughter, decimating their foes in short order, and inflicting cruel reprisals on them. But the resistance at Ashur is most stubborn.

Ashurdan is concerned the rebels might prevail. He summons his great ones and addresses them. "Great ones, you know of the desperate situation at Ashur. I seek your counsel. Speak."

A great one says, "Great and honorable king, summon garrisons from other cities and deploy them to Ashur to reinforce the Nineveh and Nimrud forces already fighting there."

"Not possible," said Ashurdan. "There are rumors of more uprisings in several major cities. I cannot afford to dwindle their garrisons. That could give our foes the opportunity for more rebellion. With the violence at many places throughout the land, it is hard to find reinforcements."

Another great one says, "Great and honorable king, perhaps we can bribe the rebels? Maybe allow them to leave the country if they desist from further fighting? I think they can find asylum in Babylon."

"What nonsense!" exclaimed another great one. "That is capitulation. We must never do that. We must fight in every way we can for as long as it takes to defeat the rebels. If we capitulate, word will spread throughout the land, and more revolts will follow. Why, in no time at all, our great nation could be reduced to a weak conglomeration of city-states. Great and honorable king, we must fight on to victory."

Ashurdan says, "Not possible. We do not have the armed forces needed for prolonged war, whether it be civil war or otherwise. We still suffer the consequences of pestilence. Our resources are depleted in every way. No, we need to find a solution that does not entail prolonged war."

Another great one says, "Great and honorable king, the rebels might be just as weary of the fight as we are. Send an emissary to Ashur to negotiate a truce."

Ashurdan says, "I did send an emissary to negotiate a truce a few weeks ago, but the rebels sent his head back to me in a basket." Frustrated by the hollow counsel he was getting, Ashurdan dismisses his great ones with no solution to his predicament.

And so, the revolt in Ashur dragged on. The combined garrisons of Nineveh and Nimrud could not suppress the revolt in the usual lightning war that Assyria is used to waging.

News of the revolt reaches the people of Nineveh. They speak of it as they encounter each other in the main square. One fellow asks, "Should we be concerned about the violence in Ashur? Can it spread to our city?"

Another fellow says, "We are fortunate here. We have peace. We have food. The great gods are protecting us. I am confident the violence will not reach us."

Another fellow says, "I am concerned that our great god of war Ashur has not smitten the revolt in the city that bears his name."

Another fellow asks, "What about the total solar eclipse we saw last year? We know it is an omen of doom for Nineveh. Did the danger really pass after the authorities completed the ritual of the substitute king? Could it be that the revolt in Ashur is a prelude to the calamity foretold by the eclipse? I am not confident about our safety."

𒀭𒂖 𒀭𒌋

It is the year of Nabukinuzur in the chronicles of the kings of Assyria. King Ashurdan recently appointed Nabukinuzur, Adorina's father, governor and high official of the great city of Nineveh. The new governor was honored by having a year named after him in the chronicles of the kings of Assyria.

Things got worse that year. The revolt in Ashur dragged on. Moreover, a violent revolt broke out in Arbaha, a city southeast of Nineveh. Messengers reported the revolt to Ashurdan. As before, he summoned his great ones for counsel. "What can I do?" asked Ashurdan. "I am constrained by a lack of resources. Speak."

The great ones gave him the same hollow advice as before, and Ashurdan dismissed it as before. Assyria continued to decline as the nation sank deeper into tribulation.

News of the revolt in Arbaha reaches the people of Nineveh. They chat about it during encounters in the main square. For the second year in a row, the people are concerned violence may come to their great city.

A fellow says, "We now have revolts in Ashur and Arbaha. I am concerned the violence could spread to our city. How long before Nineveh is threatened?"

Another fellow asks, "Must we still fear the destruction foretold by the recent solar eclipse?"

Another fellow asks, "Should we leave our homes and move to another city?"

There are those who insist on blaming families for not offering their children to the gods. "We must offer our children to the great gods," said a priest. "Those who selfishly refuse to give their children to the gods are to blame for the calamities that afflict our land. If they persist in withholding their children, we will forfeit our divine protection, and the violence will spread to our city."

The year ends worse than it began, and there is no end in sight to the calamities afflicting Assyria.

𒀭 𒂍𒁹 𒀭𒌝

It is the year of Laqipu in the chronicles of the kings of Assyria. The revolt in Arbaha drags on with no end in sight. The people of Nineveh perceive the continuing and worsening news as foretelling doom for their great city. Ninevites strolling through the main square talk among themselves. For the third year in a row, the people are concerned violence may come to their great city.

"What is going on?" asked a fellow. "I thought all things would return to normal after our great and honorable king returned from hiding."

"I thought the same," said another fellow. "Clearly, the danger to our country has not passed. Did the authorities make a mistake? Did they bring the king back too soon?"

Another fellow says, "Maybe the great gods were not pleased with the substitute king and queen they sacrificed. Those two really were of little value. Should they have chosen a more worthy pair to give to the gods?"

"No," said another fellow. "Every time they performed the ritual in the past, they chose substitutes from the rabble. Why would they do things differently this time?"

"But these are not ordinary times," said another fellow. "These extraordinary times call for extraordinary measures."

"It is time to start thinking seriously about leaving this city," said another fellow. "The rural areas might be safer places to live."

A woman turns to her husband and asks, "Should we leave our homes and our way of life? Where can we go?"

An overconfident fellow says, "Things may be bad in other parts of the country, but in Nineveh, life is good. Our economy remains strong. Jobs are plentiful. And there is peace in our city. Besides, who really knows how good or how bad things are in the rest of the land? My house chooses to stay in Nineveh."

CHAPTER 4

PLAGUES IN THE LAND

It is the year of Pan-Assur-La-Mur in the chronicles of the kings of Assyria. A violent revolt breaks out in the city of Gozan, west of Nineveh. With unrest in Ashur to the south, Arbaha to the southeast, and Gozan to the west, the Ninevites perceive a circle of violence is starting to build around their great city.

Another round of pestilence rolls across the land. Ashurdan receives reports of growing mountains of dead people, cattle, and farm animals in several cities. Scarce resources are getting scarcer. Famine, poverty, and death are crippling the nation. More violence and food riots loom.

Ashurdan summons his great ones to seek their counsel. They give him the same hollow advice as before, and he dismisses them with no solution to his predicament. Ashurdan cries out to the great gods of Assyria, "I have lost control of my country. Why is this happening? I tried to be a good and just king. What must I do to restore the favor of the great gods to my country?" Ashurdan hears utter silence, for he is crying out to idols that cannot see, hear, or speak.

Although calamity had not yet reached Nineveh, the Ninevites' confidence eroded when they heard the bad news from Gozan. For the fourth year in a row, the people are concerned violence may come to their great city. The prospect of violence is compounded by the unfolding plague. By now the people of Nineveh are starting to believe that their great gods are not so great after all. They discuss things among themselves when they meet in the main square.

"Where are our gods of healing?" asked one fellow. "Is there no end to the plagues and dying?"

"Where is our great god of war Ashur?" asked another fellow. "Why has he not smitten our enemies if he really is our great god of war? Why has he not smitten the rebels in the city that bears his name?"

"Where are our gods of prosperity?" asked another fellow. "Two plagues brought poverty and death to our land. There is violence in Ashur, Arbaha, and Gozan. More violence may arise, causing even more poverty and death."

"When will the violence reach our city?" asked another fellow. "How much longer will our great city stand?"

A priest who happened to be passing by overheard and said, "Fault lies with those who do not sacrifice enough to our great gods. It is time to stop sacrificing birds, lambs, goats, and cattle. We must sacrifice our children to the great gods."

"How terrible!" exclaimed a mother holding her newborn child in her arms. "How can we give our children to be slaughtered like animals? That is the most atrocious thing I ever heard!"

"Woman," said the priest, "it is selfish mothers like you who are to blame because you withhold your children from our great gods. Do you not know that your children do not belong to you? They belong to the great gods, they belong to Assyria, they belong to all of us. You should be ashamed for withholding your child.

The gods crave for the blood of your child. Give your child to the gods!" The mother fled in tears with her child in her arms.

Panic begins to spread in Nineveh. Some wealthy Ninevites are packing their goods and departing from the great city. Over the next several days, caravans of loaded camels, horses, donkeys, and wagons exit through the city gates. The poor remain behind with nowhere to go.

Nabukinuzur is very concerned. He addresses his great ones at his palace. "My esteemed great ones, we all know times are hard and harder times are coming. Assyria faces great and seemingly insurmountable challenges. But we are a great people of the greatest city on the earth. We will get through this. So far, the impact of the recent calamities has been minimal in our city. But I think it is only a matter of time before our national crisis engulfs Nineveh. Our great and honorable King Ashurdan is paralyzed by an endless stream of dreadful developments. We are enduring a tribulation of plagues, portent in the heavens, war, and rumors of war. The people's confidence in our great gods has fallen to an all-time low; many fear our nation is imploding. People are fleeing the city in fear of the doom foretold by the great solar eclipse. But we must not abandon our own people, even if it means enduring hardship and tribulation alongside them. I still believe Assyria will be saved. I believe so because I have great confidence in you and our people. Perhaps the great gods have protected Nineveh to position us to lead the way out of our national crisis. If we rise to the challenge and succeed, generations will honor us for a thousand years. But if we cower and fail, generations will despise us for a thousand years. Whether it is by fate or divine providence, here we stand. As they say, as goes Nineveh, so goes Assyria."

The great ones applauded Nabukinuzur's speech. One by one they pledged to stand with him to the very end, all except Muska, a priest of the great gods. He had another agenda in mind.

Adorina usually sits quietly at gatherings of the governor and his great ones, a practice most of them frown on. She sat through her father's speech and heartily congratulated him.

"Father, I pledge to do all within my power to help you succeed in your endeavor. But Father, are we seeking the true God in all this? You know I had a Hebrew tutor several years ago. He taught me science, astronomy, mathematics, history, and philosophy. But from time to time, he also spoke to me of his Hebrew God, who is not like our gods of wood, stone, and metal. He is pure spirit. He is all-good, all-knowing, and all-powerful. He is appalled by cruelty and injustice. Unlike our idols of wood, stone, and metal, he really sees, hears, and speaks. In my heart, I believe the Hebrew God really is God. I also believe he is outraged over the endless cruelties committed by several of our kings during their ruthless wars of conquest. I believe retribution is coming to Assyria on account of those endless cruelties. I believe the Hebrew God is chastising our land. My father, if Assyria is to be saved, the nation must repent of her past misdeeds and her current sinfulness. Maybe the reason Nineveh is still standing is because the Hebrew God is giving us space to repent for the entire nation."

"My daughter, you are a dreamer," said Nabukinuzur. "Your heart is good, but you must come down to earth and live in the real world. The only real god in this world, the one god all people submit to whether they want to or not, is power. Assyria wields real power over the earth. If the Hebrew god is all-powerful, why did he let Assyria trample the nations for over half a millennium? Either he is not all-powerful, or he does not even exist. I fear your old Hebrew tutor filled your head with fantasies."

"I think not, Father," said Adorina. "There really is something to the Hebrew teachings about their God. I believe he is real and is at work in the world today. I also believe that if Assyria does not change her ways, there will be a day of reckoning for the nation. These terrible things that are happening in our land, are they isolated and unrelated events, or are they evidence of divine judgment over Assyria?"

Nabukinuzur replied, "Daughter, you believe what you want, but as far as I am concerned, you are deceived by folly. Moreover, be careful not to speak against our king, our nation, or our great gods." At that, Nabukinuzur departed to his living quarters.

𒅀 𒂊𒀉 𒅀𒌍

It is the year of Bel-Taggil in the chronicles of the kings of Assyria. There are faint rumblings of spiritual awakening in Nineveh. Some people are turning away from the great gods of Assyria. A few are seeking to know the true God.

Adorina is one of the few. One day, she speaks to Rabbu about the true God while playing the Royal Game of Ur at her house. "Rabbu, do you believe in the true God?"

"There are many gods," said Rabbu. "Does not each nation have its own god or even several gods, as does Assyria?" he asked.

"But do you believe there is a God above all, a good God who hates the injustices of the world, who promises to fix this fallen world one day?" she asked.

Rabbu pauses to think, and then replies, "I saw many horrible things during my military service. I saw dreadful massacres. I killed men ruthlessly in battle. I helped the king's army lay waste to entire cities and enslave their populations. I did it all for the glory of the great gods, for my king, and for my country. Yet I now grieve over the things I saw and did. At times I wonder. Is there a true God out there, and is he speaking to my soul? Is he telling me that I need to be forgiven for my past?"

"Deep in your heart, you do believe in him, Rabbu," said Adorina.

"Maybe I do; maybe I do not," said Rabbu. "But the more I see of this world, the harder I find it to believe in a good and all-powerful God. Even so, I wonder." Rabbu looks at the game board and notices Adorina's game pieces had outmaneuvered his game pieces. "You beat me again," he said.

"Come, let us enjoy a fresh cup of wine and talk some more," said Adorina. She takes Rabbu's arm and leads him to the dining room. As happens every time he is with Adorina, Rabbu's heart pounds mightily. He never wants these precious moments with Adorina to end.

𒀭 𒂠𒁲 𒀭𒀪

Something very sinister is brewing in Kuyunjik, the hilly district of Nineveh where the grand temples of the great gods stand high above the city. A new fellow has become the high priest of Ishtar at the great temple that bears her name. His name is Malkuno. He is an exceptionally vile, cruel, and inhuman fellow. He is tall, robust, and heavyset. He has the face of a lizard with beady eyes, long white hair, and a long white beard, and he always displays a menacing scowl on his reptilian face. It is said that his mother gave birth to him after mating with a creature that crawled out of a haunted dark lagoon.

Malkuno spent many years in Canaan before coming to Assyria. While living in Canaan, he fought for the heathen nations and served their heathen gods. He was a mighty swordsman. With a single stroke of his huge broadsword, he would cleave an armored foe in two, lengthwise. It is said he is mightier than the great Goliath of the Philistines. Malkuno became rich by kidnapping young children and selling them to priests of Baal for sacrifice at the high places.

It is said Malkuno is immortal. Legend has it he was killed in battle years ago. Upon dying, his soul was sentenced to eternity in hell for his innumerable foul deeds. But so evil and wicked was he that even the devil of hell would not withstand him. The devil expelled Malkuno from hell and sent him back to earth.

In his lust for power and wealth, Malkuno decided that the best way to gain both is to rule over the greatest city on the earth. "There is no greater city to rule than the great city of Nineveh," said Malkuno to himself. And so, he masterminded a plan to become ruler of Nineveh. He would make himself high priest of a great god of Assyria and use that position to delude the Ninevites to submit to his will.

Malkuno said to himself, "The favorite great gods of the Ninevites are the storm god Adad, the war god Ashur, and the goddess of war and fertility Ishtar. If I can convince the Ninevites to make me high priest of one of these, I can set myself up to rule the great city of Nineveh. Which will it be? The storm god Adad? No. Adad is to Assyria what Baal was to Canaan. The armies of Yahweh under the command of Joshua defeated the nations of Baal many times. Thus, Baal was not so great. Likewise, Adad cannot be so great. Ashur? No. The priesthood of Ashur is too powerful and exclusive to infiltrate. Ishtar? Yes! The Queen of Heaven! The cult of Ishtar grew even as the imperial might of Assyria grew. The Assyrians made her the nation's goddess of nature, passion, fertility, sex, war, and healing. What a magnificent combination! If I become her high priest, I can manipulate and control the people."

He continues to lay out his scheme. "As high priest of the Queen of Heaven, I may also influence the priesthood of Ashur. Ishtar has many priestesses. I will tout my experience serving the gods of Canaan to persuade the Ninevites that an all-male priesthood of Ishtar will bring greater glory to the city. I will persuade them to commission me to restructure the priesthood of Ishtar. I will remove all the priestesses and appoint loyal male friends as priests. My new priestly friends will be indebted to me. Then I will convince them to reward me by installing me as high priest. Hence, I will be positioned to exploit the superstitions and religious traditions of Assyria. I will be able to manipulate the people and gain absolute power over Nineveh. What will be the most effective superstition to exploit? Child sacrifice? Yes! The Assyrians already sacrifice children to Adad and Ishtar. I will convince them that increased and intensified child sacrifice will make the great city even greater. I know they will fall for it just like the Canaanites did before the days of Yahweh. In time, I may even exalt myself as a god over Nineveh. I will make the people bow down and worship me. All that oppose me, I will put to death without pity. Who knows what might come next? Someday I may even be exalted as a god over the entire Assyrian Empire and hence over the entire world!"

Malkuno came to Nineveh and implemented his devious and crafty plan. Over time, he seduced hundreds of influential Ninevites to become his supporters. They elevated him to the exalted position of high priest of Ishtar. Malkuno promptly exploited his newfound power and made himself even more powerful by liberal use of bribery, intimidation, extortion, and murder. In this year of Bel-Taggil, Malkuno is within reach of his goal.

Immortal or not, Malkuno serves the darkest powers. The sacred precinct of Ishtar in Nineveh is his corner of the world. The fiery altar of Ishtar is Malkuno's man-made hell on earth. The priests and temple guards serve him as his lackeys; they are his cult following.

One day, Malkuno and his cult followers meet at the temple of Ishtar to devise a plan to seize absolute power over Nineveh. "Times are bad in Assyria," he said. "At times like these, it is easier to convince the people to follow us. We will tell them the tribulation the nation is going through is the fault of those who withhold their children from the great gods. We will convince them that our intercession with the gods will save the nation. We will stir the masses to demand that parents give up their children to the gods. When the time is right, we will roam through the city and seize young children and bring them here to be sacrificed. The temple guards will accompany us, armed as needed in case we encounter resistance. Moreover, we can stir up mobs to support us. We will hire local ruffians and pay them with gold and silver from the temple offerings. After a while, the people will surrender more power to us, and we will rule Nineveh."

"Your plan is good, Lord Malkuno," said a priest of Ishtar. "But what if after the people obey us, things get worse instead of better? What then? Might they turn against us?"

"No," replied Malkuno. "We just tell the people things are getting worse because they are not sacrificing enough. People are stupid. They will fall for it. Trust me. I have a lot of experience in these things from my days serving the gods of Canaan."

Another priest of Ishtar spoke. "Lord Malkuno, we may have a problem with Nabukinuzur, the governor and high official of Nineveh. It is said he is a just and honest ruler who hates lawlessness and mobs. He is committed to the rule of law. If there is no law that justifies our actions, he will oppose us. What then?"

Then another priest spoke. "I heard about this Nabukinuzur. They say he is so foolish he would never condemn a man to death without first granting him a fair trial. What a dupe! Why should anyone with at least half a mind care about fairness?"

Then another priest spoke. "We may need to dispose of Nabukinuzur. We can hire an assassin to kill him. We tell the people he was murdered by an enemy of the great gods. Then we tell them they must sacrifice their children to atone for the crime.

I am sure they will fall for it. We can even recruit for our mob from among the people who believe our story. They can help us snatch children."

Then another priest spoke. "I hear that Nabukinuzur's daughter, Adorina, often pleads with her father to show mercy to the accused. The humble people of Nineveh admire her. They see her as their protector. Moreover, she speaks against the sacrificial rites of the temples. Perhaps we can bring up charges of blasphemy against her and have her executed. That will bring disgrace to Nabukinuzur. He will have to step down. When he does, we convince the king he must appoint as governor whoever the gods say. We tell him the gods told us who they want as governor, and we give the king the name of someone loyal to us."

"Your suggestion is reasonable," said Malkuno, "but I prefer a more direct approach. When it comes to solving problems, there is nothing more direct than an assassin's dagger. My fellow priests, prepare plans to implement the things we discussed. Set aside temple gold and silver to hire ruffians and bribe our friends."

An old woman who sweeps the temple floors overheard the plotting. That night, she went to Adorina's house. She made sure no one followed her. The old woman knocked on the door and a servant girl opened the door. The servant brought her before Adorina. The old woman asked, "Lady, do you remember me?"

Adorina looked closely at her and said, "Yes, I remember you. You served at my father's house when I was a little girl. Why have you come?"

"Lady, these days I sweep the floors of the temple of Ishtar at Kuyunjik. This past day I overheard some wicked plotting in the temple. Malkuno, the new high priest, is planning evil against the governor and you. I heard talk of hiring an assassin."

"I believe you, and I will heed your warning," said Adorina. "I have heard about Malkuno from others, none of it good. My father is already suspicious of him. Here, receive these gold coins, which I give you in gratitude for warning me."

"No, dear lady," said the old woman. "You need not reward me. Your father and you were kind to me. I want no evil to befall you."

"Please accept the coins anyway," said Adorina. "If you have no need of them, you can share with the poor."

"Thank you, dear lady," said the old woman.

"Go in peace," said Adorina.

The old woman departed from Adorina's house. But while she took precautions to avoid being followed on her way to the house, it did not occur to her to take precautions to avoid being followed as she went away. Malkuno had already sent a loyal follower to spy on Adorina's house. The spy followed the old woman as she left. When he discovered her house, he went to the temple of Ishtar and reported to Malkuno.

That very night, temple guards went to the old woman's house and seized her. They took the coins Adorina gave her, and they dragged her off to the temple and brought her before Malkuno. The temple guards showed him the gold coins she received from Adorina. Malkuno stared at the old woman with his beady eyes and said, "You wretched old woman! I see you spied for the governor's daughter. That will cost you your life. Men, take these coins and add them to the assassin's purse."

"What of the old woman?" asked a temple guard.

"Kill her," replied Malkuno, with a reptilian smile on his face.

Then the old woman spoke. "Malkuno, you are evil. One day, you will pay for your crimes. A higher power will judge you, and there will be no escape for you."

"How dare you speak to me like that, you despicable and pathetic old woman?" shouted Malkuno. "I am the higher power. Do you understand? I am the higher power! I was going to slit your throat, but that is too merciful for you. Guard, draw your dagger and cut out her tongue. Then throw her into the gaping pit of fire in the altar room." The old woman screamed in terror as the guard grabbed her and cut out her tongue. Then she could scream no more. The guard threw her over his shoulder, carried her to the altar room, and dropped her into the gaping pit of fire.

CHAPTER 5

AN INTERRUPTED JOURNEY

Jonah, son of Amittai, is an anointed prophet of the Most High in the northern kingdom of Israel, which is ruled by King Jeroboam. Jonah walks in the spirit of Elijah. It is a day like any other as Jonah goes about his usual business. Unknown to him, this day is destined to become a day like no other.

Jonah hears the word of the Most High: *"Go to the great city of Nineveh and preach against it, because its wickedness has come up before me"* (Jonah 1:2). Jonah dreads going to Nineveh because he despises the Assyrians. Jonah is keenly aware of the horrors the Assyrians inflicted on conquered lands during their relentless and ruthless westward expansion toward the Great Sea. The atrocities committed by the Assyrian kings Ashurnasirpal and Shalmaneser are known by all. It was Shalmaneser who humiliated King Ahab of Israel by defeating him and his eleven allies at the battle of Karkar about a hundred years ago. The ever-expanding Assyrian Empire has already fought its way to the eastern edge of the Great Sea; Assyrian regiments in Lebanon are dangerously close to Israel's northern border.

Jonah decides he will not go to Assyria. Instead, he goes down to the port city of Joppa on the eastern edge of the Great Sea and finds a ship bound for Tarshish, a city at the far western end of the world. Jonah believes that the Most High will not find him there. He pays the fare and boards the ship. The weather is good, and the ship sets sail. It is a day like any other for the sailors manning the ship. Unknown to them, it is destined to become a day like no other.

The Most High chastens Jonah for his disobedience:

> *Then the LORD sent a great wind on the sea, and such a violent storm arose that the ship threatened to break up. All the sailors were afraid and each cried out to his own god. And they threw the cargo into the sea to lighten the ship. But Jonah had gone below deck, where he lay down and fell into a deep sleep. The captain went to him and said, "How can you sleep? Get up and call on your god! Maybe he will take notice of us so that we will not perish."*
>
> *Then the sailors said to each other, "Come, let us cast lots to find out who is responsible for this calamity." They cast lots and the lot fell on Jonah. So they asked him, "Tell us, who is responsible for making all this trouble for us? What kind of work do you do? Where do you come from? What is your country? From what people are you?"*
>
> *He answered, "I am a Hebrew and I worship the LORD, the God of heaven, who made the sea and the dry land." This terrified them and they asked, "What have you done?" (They knew he was running away from the LORD, because he had already told them so.) The sea was getting rougher and rougher. So*

they asked him, "What should we do to you to make the sea calm down for us?"

"Pick me up and throw me into the sea," he replied, "and it will become calm. I know that it is my fault that this great storm has come upon you."

Instead, the men did their best to row back to land. But they could not, for the sea grew even wilder than before. Then they cried out to the LORD, "Please, LORD, do not let us die for taking this man's life. Do not hold us accountable for killing an innocent man, for you, LORD, have done as you pleased." Then they took Jonah and threw him overboard, and the raging sea grew calm. At this the men greatly feared the LORD, and they offered a sacrifice to the LORD and made vows to him.

—Jonah 1:4–16

Jonah descends into the depths of the Great Sea. He holds his breath for as long as he can, even as he expects to die by drowning. The water grows darker and colder as he sinks. Then he sees a huge dark mass approaching him. He does not know what it is. He thinks, *"Maybe the dark mass is the spirit of death coming for me. Maybe I am hallucinating."* Suddenly, the dark mass engulfs Jonah. He feels a sudden rush of water, and his head emerges above water. Jonah can breathe at last, and he rejoices. But he has no idea what has engulfed him, for he is immersed in pitch-black darkness.

There is a strong odor of fish all around him. He senses he is moving, as if the dark mass is carrying him along. Then he sees a hole opening in front of him. The light of day shines through the hole, and Jonah sees the sky and the clouds. He notices he is in a shallow pool of water and seaweed. The opening hole looks like the mouth of a fish. Suddenly, Jonah realizes he is inside the belly of a huge fish. He says to himself, *"I expected to die by drowning, but the Lord sent a huge fish to rescue me from the depths that I might not perish. What an amazing rescue!"*

For three days and three nights, Jonah travels in the belly of the fish. He prays to the Most High:

> *In my distress I called to the LORD, and he answered me. From deep in the realm of the dead I called for help, and you listened to my cry. You hurled me into the depths, into the very heart of the seas, and the currents swirled about me; all your waves and breakers swept over me. I said, "I have been banished from your sight; yet I will look again toward your holy temple." The engulfing waters threatened me, the deep surrounded me; seaweed was wrapped around my head. To the roots of the mountains I sank down; the earth beneath barred me in forever. But you, LORD my God, brought my life up from the pit. When my life was ebbing away, I remembered you, LORD, and my prayer rose to you, to your holy temple. Those who cling to worthless idols turn away from God's love for them. But I, with shouts of grateful praise, will sacrifice to you. What I have vowed I will make good. I will say, "Salvation comes from the LORD."*
>
> —Jonah 2:2–9

𒌋𒁹 �----- 𒌋𒁹𒌍

Eliab and his son Abidan are fishing at the eastern shoreline of the Great Sea. Their day began like any other. Unknown to them, they are destined to receive a visitor like no other.

Abidan notices a strange sight in the water. "Father, look out there," he said. "Do you see that strange thing approaching the shore?"

"I do, son," said Eliab.

"Is it a sea monster?" asked Abidan.

"I do not know, son," replied Eliab. "But step back from the water. It seems to be headed straight for us, and it might be dangerous."

Eliab and Abidan step back a safe distance from the water's edge. A giant fish swims to the very edge of the water, opens its mouth, and discharges a stream of water, seaweed, and what appears to be a live man. Then the fish turns around and swims back out to the open sea.

"Father," cried Abidan, "that man is alive!"

"Son, come help me lift him up," said Eliab.

Eliab and Abidan run to the man and lift him from a shallow pool of water and seaweed. The man has a strong smell of fish all over him. Eliab speaks to him. "I am Eliab, and this is my son Abidan. We live in that village you see over there."

The man slowly rises to his feet. Eliab asks, "Who are you? How do you feel? Do you have enough strength to stand?"

The man replies, "I am Jonah, a Hebrew. I feel good and I have enough strength to stand and walk."

"How did you come to be inside that monstrous fish?" asked Eliab.

Jonah replies, "I was on a ship bound for Tarshish. The Lord sent a great storm upon the sea because I was running from him. I told the sailors that if they throw me overboard, the Lord would calm the sea. They did, and the sea calmed; that giant fish swallowed me and rescued me from drowning."

"God must have a great task for you, Jonah," said Eliab. "You must be hungry, thirsty, and tired. Come to my house, bathe, eat, drink, and be refreshed. Then you can tell us more about your most unusual journey."

Eliab brings Jonah to his house. "Jonah, this is my wife, Miriam."

"What in the world happened to you, Jonah?" asked Miriam. "Forgive me for saying so, but you look and smell like you just crawled out of the belly of a fish."

Eliab and Abidan laugh. "He did, Miriam," said Eliab.

"What?" asked Miriam. "Did you just come up with a fish story?"

"No, Miriam," said Eliab. "Jonah will explain everything. But first, pour some water for him to drink and prepare a meal for him. He can bathe while the food is cooking. We should boil his clothes."

"Boil his clothes?" asked Miriam. "Better that we burn them. We have spare clothing he can wear."

Jonah spends the night in Eliab's house. The entire household gathers at the dinner table with Jonah. "Tell me, Jonah, just what is this grand mission from God that caused you to flee to Tarshish?" asked Eliab.

Jonah replies, "The Lord commanded me to go at once to Nineveh, that great city, and preach against it, for their wickedness has come up before him."

"You are to preach against the Assyrians?" asked Eliab. "That is madness. Do you not know of the extreme cruelty of the Assyrians? What do you think they will do to you if you preach against them in their great city? You could be arrested and thrown into a dungeon. You could be fed to the lions, hyaenas, and jackals roaming the land. You could be slain as a sacrifice to their gods. You could even be burned alive."

Jonah replies, "I am aware of the extreme cruelty of the Assyrians. That is why I did not want to go to Nineveh. I feared the Lord might forgive them if they repent at my preaching. I want them to perish. But there will be no more running from the Lord for me."

Miriam serves a platter of broiled meat, fresh vegetables, and bread. They say a prayer of thanksgiving to the Most High. Then

Jonah says, "Thank you too, dear lady, for not serving fish of the sea." All laugh at Jonah's witty remark.

The next day, Eliab has some good news. "Jonah, a caravan of merchants just arrived at our village. They are on their way to Persia. I was told they plan to stop at Nineveh on the way and do commerce in the great city. You should ride with them. It is a long road to Nineveh, and there will be bandits and wild beasts along the way. You can travel under the protection of the caravan."

"But I have no money to pay my way," said Jonah.

"Here," said Eliab. "We took up a collection for you in the village. There is enough money to pay for the trip to Nineveh."

"Thank you very much, Eliab," said Jonah. "The Lord bless you and keep you. I want to thank the villagers for their generosity."

"No time to do so," said Eliab. "The caravan leaves as soon as their horses and donkeys are watered. Come, I will introduce you to the caravan master. He will let you ride on a camel. Have you ever been on a camel? It is tricky to avoid falling off as its hump sways from side to side while walking."

Jonah says, "Better than being thrown into a rough sea."

The caravan is ready to leave. Jonah mounts a camel with help from some riders. In a few moments the caravan begins to move. Eliab waves farewell to Jonah, fearing this will be a one-way trip for his new friend. Then Eliab raises his hands toward heaven and prays, "Lord God of Abraham, Isaac, and Israel, bless and protect your servant Jonah."

The village children laugh as they watch Jonah ride. They are amused by the difficulty he has staying on the camel while its hump sways from side to side.

One evening during a rest stop for meals, some merchants question Jonah. "Is it true you are going to preach against the Ninevites? The Assyrians are a violent people who worship bloodthirsty gods of war. They will kill you."

The caravan master says to Jonah, "You can ride with us until we are within sight of the great city. At that moment, you will fall back and keep some distance between you and us. If you get into trouble in Nineveh, which you most surely will, I do not want them to know you came with us."

That night, Jonah had a frightening dream. He was standing before the entrance to a grand hall. Two gigantic lamassus stood at the entrance, facing outward. Both stood on elaborate pedestals. One lamassu appeared to come alive. It turned its head toward Jonah and growled at him. Then the lamassu leaped off its pedestal and lurched toward Jonah. Fear overcame him, and he ran away. But the lamassu pursued Jonah relentlessly as he ran down a long corridor. When he reached the end of the corridor, he saw that he was trapped, with no way out. The lamassu drew near, growling ever louder. It opened its mouth wide and lurched its head forward to devour Jonah. He thought, *"The Lord who rescued me from the depths of the raging sea can rescue me from the jaws of this raging lamassu. But will he?"* At that moment, a lightning bolt struck the lamassu, shattering it into a thousand smoldering pieces. Then Jonah woke up sweating.

𒅓 𒂄 𒅓𒌋

After a long trek along the Way of the Sea, that well-traveled highway from Egypt to the fertile crescent, the caravan is within sight of the great city. "Jonah," said the caravan master, "here we part company. Go with God."

Jonah dismounts and stands alone beside the road as the caravan moves on toward the open gate of the great city. After allowing some distance between himself and the caravan, he begins his lonely walk to the gates of Nineveh.

Jonah is appalled by what he sees as he approaches the great city. Even from afar, he sees the ziggurats, the multi-layered temples of the great gods of Assyria, towering high above the city walls. Jonah dreads entering the great city. Troubling thoughts flow through his mind:

> "The city has outward beauty. It almost looks like a nice place to live, except for the bloodguilt of her many ruthless wars of conquest and the hideous idolatry and abominable practices of her awesome temples. Those temples are homes to gods of war and child sacrifice. So many magnificent temples, all raised up to worthless idols—gods that cannot see, hear, or speak—each housed in a temple like the tower of Babel in days of old. What horrible demon gods do these people worship? I see smoke rising from a temple. What hideous rites are they performing there? Child sacrifice to the Baals? Child sacrifice to the Queen of Heaven? Is that smoke all that remains of children given to the gods of Assyria? How could God send me to this despicable city?"

As he draws near the open gate, Jonah notices a tiny village by the side of the road. An old man is sitting on a rock at the entrance to the village. The old man looks straight at Jonah, and Jonah immediately discerns the old man has the spirit of prophecy. The old man speaks to Jonah. "The spirit of Elijah be upon you, sir."

Jonah says, "The spirit of Elijah be upon you too, sir. Do you prophesy to the people of the great city?"

The old man replies, "I heal the sick and comfort the suffering among travelers who come and go, but I have never entered the great city. Do you come to prophesy to the city?"

Jonah replies, "Yes, with reluctance. But I choose to obey the Lord despite my misgivings. Even so, I feel overcome sometimes by fear and anxiety over my mission."

The old man asks, "What is God's word for the great city?"

"That the wickedness of this city has reached heaven, and in forty more days, Nineveh will be overthrown," replied Jonah.

The old man says, "My brother, your challenge is great, but we serve a greater God. Come to my house and share a meal with me and be refreshed before entering the city." Jonah accepts the invitation. He spends some time with the old man and then resumes his journey.

Jonah approaches the open gate along with some merchants seeking to do commerce in the great city. He notices fierce-looking Assyrian soldiers on the city walls, arrayed in royal blue tunics and clad in heavy iron armor and conical helmets. The soldiers notice Jonah. They stare at him with intimidating looks. Fearful thoughts flow through Jonah's mind. *"Any moment, one of those soldiers might hurl a spear at me and thus end my mission right here and now."* But there is no turning back, no running from the Most High this time. Trusting in divine protection, he proceeds through the open gate. Once inside, Jonah makes his way to the main square of the city, convinced it is a good place to begin preaching.

Jonah contemplates the multitudes at the city square. What he sees unsettles him. Many taverns are serving intoxicating beverages. Drunken brawlers pour out of the taverns and fight in the streets, some with knives and clubs. Their violence spills over into the neighboring shops, injuring people, and damaging property. Thieves raid the damaged shops. Sometimes, they beat up the already injured shopkeepers before running off with their wares. There are several brothels. Scantily clad Ninevite women display themselves shamelessly in provocative poses at the brothel doors. Some of them stare at Jonah.

One says to him, "Hey, stranger, are you looking for a good time? Come inside. Our price is fair."

Jonah ignores her and moves on. Then he sees something worse. There are many small heathen altars throughout the square. People line up to burn incense at the altars. Jonah is appalled by their acts of idolatry.

Two soldiers watch Jonah suspiciously. One soldier says, "That stranger looks like an Israelite. He could be a spy. Should we report him to the commander?"

"No," replied the other soldier. "He would be disguised if he were a spy. He is probably just a merchant. Foreigners come and go all the time. But let us watch him from a distance for a while. If he does something suspicious, we report him to the commander."

Then Jonah comes upon a sight that really frightens him. He finds himself face-to-face with a pair of colossal and imposing lamassus. They appear to be staring right at him. He moves along. But as he looks in another direction, he sees another pair of colossal and imposing lamassus. They also appear to be staring right at him. As he walks in another direction and looks back, it seems like the lamassus' eyes roll his way and follow him. He moves along and comes face-to-face with yet another pair of lamassus staring at him. He looks around again and notices that pairs of giant lamassus can be seen from all directions, and they all seem to be staring at him. Fearful thoughts flow through Jonah's mind. *"Are those stone-faced lamassus really staring at me? Are their eyes really moving and following me wherever I go? Or am I just starting to lose my mind?"*

Jonah moves on. He comes across a small group of wailing women. Jonah speaks to them. "Ladies, why are you crying? Did you lose sons or husbands in the wars?"

One woman replies, "Our children were taken from us and sacrificed at the great temple of Ishtar. Look over there." She points toward the hilly sector of Nineveh called Kuyunjik. "Do you not see the smoke rising from the temple of Ishtar? All that remains of our children is in that smoke." Jonah is horrified.

Another woman cries out, "They say Malkuno, the high priest of Ishtar, wants our children. What mother or father would want to give up their little ones to be burned at the altars of the gods?"

But not all were wailing over the loss of their children. One woman who overheard the conversation says, "You selfish women! It is people like you who bring the wrath of the great gods upon us when you withhold your children. Do you not know that your children do not belong to you? They belong to the great gods, they belong to our nation, and they belong to us. You cannot have your way with them just because you are their mothers. I, for one, have given three children to the great gods, and I will get pregnant again to give more." At those words, the wailing women cry even louder.

As Jonah decides what to do next, he thinks, "*I have seen and heard enough of the wickedness of this city and its religion. Yet I see that not all Ninevites are totally evil. Those wailing women need the peace of the Lord. But it seems that for the most part, Nineveh is a wicked, carnal, violent, idolatrous city and a haven for evil people. I am beginning to understand why the Lord sent me here. I must preach his truth to these people. A few may repent though most might not. Few or many, there are souls that can be saved here. It is time they hear the word of the Lord.*"

Jonah searches briefly for a convenient spot from which he can address the multitudes. He climbs up on the elevated balcony of a nearby building. From this new vantage point, he again sees a pair of colossal and imposing lamassus staring his way. They look as menacing as the others. He still fears them, but the time has come for the prophet to take his stand for the Most High. No more fear! Filled with the spirit of the Most High, Jonah begins to speak. "People of the great city of Nineveh, I am Jonah, a Hebrew. I worship the Lord, the God of heaven, who made the sea and the dry land. Now hear the word of the Lord! The wickedness of this city has come up before him."

Then Jonah declares God's judgment against the great city: *"Forty more days and Nineveh will be overthrown"* (Jonah 3:4).

𒅴 𒂊𒇷 𒅴𒌋

Multitudes heard Jonah preach that day. Most ignored him. A fellow said, "Philosophers, soothsayers, and prophets come and go, and nothing exciting ever happens. Let us just ignore the stranger. He is here today, gone tomorrow."

Some laughed and mocked him. "Who is that babbler that says our city will be overthrown?" asked another fellow. "There is no army in all the earth that can overthrow us."

Some reviled him. "Who is that rat who dares to threaten us?" asked another fellow. "Someone should find soldiers and have them drag him away that he may be put to death in an ignominious manner."

Some thought he was mad. "The stranger must have been standing in the sun too long," said another fellow. "He is delirious. To the madman's prison with him!"

Even so, some felt conviction. "Some of our kings were exceptionally cruel to conquered peoples," said another fellow. "If the gods are just, they cannot look indifferently upon acts of utter barbarism. I fear overdue justice may be coming our way."

Another fellow says, "Our great city is swimming in immorality. Prostitution and drunkenness are everywhere. There is murder in the streets, and corrupt officials take bribes. How long can any god who loves justice put up with this?"

Another fellow says, "Our religion is depraved. We worship bloodthirsty gods of war. We surrender our children to be sacrificed in hideous rituals. What good gods can demand these things?"

Another fellow says, "The day of reckoning for our sins draws near. Consider what has been happening these past seven years. We have had plagues and the portent of the solar eclipse, which foretells destruction of our city. We have had war and rumors of war, and the rumblings of our demise grow louder. The Hebrew speaks truth; we must listen to him and turn from our wicked ways before a terrible hammer of judgment falls on us."

A few people here and there believed Jonah. They gathered in small groups of a dozen or so to pray and appeal to the god of heaven. But as the days passed, the few groups of a dozen grew to several groups of hundreds throughout the great city. Many people began to fast. Many put on sackcloth and mourned for Nineveh. Some put sackcloth on their animals and made them partakers of mourning, as in the way of the Persians.

𒀭 𒂊𒁺 𒀭𒀸

A few days later, a military officer brings an unusual report to Nabukinuzur. "Governor, a strange Hebrew visitor is stirring the people. He calls himself Jonah and claims to be a messenger sent by his god. He is telling the people that our great city will be overthrown in forty days. I have some men following him with orders to seize him if he does anything suspicious. So far, he has not done anything overtly criminal or violent. But his words are unsettling to many."

Nabukinuzur says, "He is probably a soothsayer of some kind. They come and go all the time. Most people just ignore their babble. How long has he been in the city?"

"It has been three days since he first spoke in public," replied the officer. "In those three days, he crossed from one end of the city to the other preaching endlessly along the way."

Nabukinuzur asks, "How are the people reacting to the Hebrew?"

"Most ignore him. But some people gather in groups here and there to beseech his god," replied the officer. "Some are mourning or fasting. Most groups are small, but a few number in the hundreds."

"Is there any hint of lawlessness, violence, sedition, or treason on the part of the people?" asked Nabukinuzur.

"No," replied the officer. "The gatherings are peaceful."

"Has the Hebrew incited rebellion of any kind?" asked Nabukinuzur.

"No, governor," replied the officer. "It appears his only offense is strange preaching."

"Keep him under surveillance," said Nabukinuzur. "If he speaks against the king or if he incites violence or rebellion, bring him to me in chains. But if his only offense is strange preaching, ignore him. In time, the people will ignore him too; then he will leave the city, and it will be as if he was never here."

"We will do as you have ordered, governor," said the officer.

Palakh, Nabukinuzur's most trusted servant, overheard the conversation. "Governor, with respect, you should not take lightly the Hebrew's preaching. The total solar eclipse in the year of Esdu-Sarabe is an omen of Nineveh's destruction. Could it be the Hebrew is a messenger sent by the gods to remind us of the future destruction of Nineveh? Could it be he just revealed the precise day it will happen? He did say Nineveh will be overthrown in just forty days. Moreover, it is said the Hebrew god is a god of miracles. He has the power to destroy Nineveh even as he destroyed the infamous cities of Sodom and Gomorrah in days of old."

Nabukinuzur asks, "Was the destruction of Nineveh not canceled when the ritual of the substitute king was performed in the year of Esdu-Sarabe?"

"Maybe not," said Palakh. "Normal times have not returned to our land. The opposite is happening. Conditions in our land have worsened considerably even after our king returned from hiding. Plague, war, and rumors of war afflict our land. It appears we are in the midst of a crescendo of tribulation. I plead you consider the possibility the Hebrew is revealing our true fate."

Nabukinuzur says, "Palakh, my most trusted servant, if it were not for the foreboding events of the past few years, I would have dismissed your words as nonsense. But there is at least the possibility that you are right. I need to think about this more. Meanwhile, we will keep our eyes on the Hebrew and try to find out as much as we can about him. But of this I am sure: Our great gods are greater than the Hebrew's god. They will see us through this tribulation. When all this is over, no one will remember that Hebrew's visit to Nineveh."

CHAPTER 6

THEY ARE COMING FOR THE CHILDREN

Some hearts were hardened at the preaching of Jonah. One night, Malkuno and his cult followers meet in secret at the temple of Ishtar. "We must dispose of that Hebrew rabble-rouser," said Malkuno. "He is turning people away from our great gods to his god of goats, camels, and slaves. We cannot allow that. Who will be left to follow us if the Hebrew keeps turning the people away? I say we find some ruffians who are willing to murder him for a bag of gold or silver coins."

"I agree," said a priest of Ishtar. "Let us hire someone to slit his throat."

"I know where we can find the talent we need," said another priest. "Give me a bag of twenty gold or silver coins, and I will return with an assassin suitable for our purpose."

"That sounds like a good plan," said Malkuno. "Here, take this bag of coins. It should be enough. Go and recruit our assassin. We will meet here again tomorrow morning. Bring the assassin to the meeting, and we will give him instructions."

The next morning, Malkuno and his cult followers meet again in secret at the temple of Ishtar. A priest introduces three ruffians he recruited as assassins. "Lord Malkuno and fellow priests of the Queen of Heaven, meet Aho, Gewargis, and Nuhro," he said. "As you can see, they are big, tough, and mean. For a single bag of thirty gold coins, they will dispose of the Hebrew. They have done this sort of thing before. They are very good at what they do, and they always work together. Lord Malkuno, do you agree to their price?"

"I do," said Malkuno. "Aho, Gewargis, and Nuhro, what is your plan?"

As ringleader of the trio, Aho replied, "Lord Malkuno, this Hebrew preaches to the people every day in public, so it will be easy to find him by day. Then we will follow him stealthily to wherever he rests at night. There we will slit his throat."

"Good plan," said Malkuno. "Proceed and report back here after you kill the Hebrew. I trust you will also dispose of his body?"

"Most certainly, Lord Malkuno," replied Aho. "After we are done with that Hebrew, it will be as if he never lived."

𒅑 𒂡 𒅑𒌋

Later that day, Adorina heard Jonah preach. She spoke to him. "Sir, I am a Ninevite of noble birth. I am loyal to my country, but I despise some of the things happening in my country and in my city. The violence and cruelty of some of our kings must be reckoned with. Violence and immorality run strong in this city. I grieve for Nineveh. As a young girl, I was tutored by a fine Hebrew teacher who taught me the moral law of your God. I believe your God is all-good, all-knowing, and all-powerful. I believe you are a true prophet of his, and I want your mission here to succeed."

"Dear lady, the Lord's truth is in your heart," said Jonah. "Are there many here who believe as you?"

"Not many," said Adorina. "But the number grows each day. Now tell me, sir, if the people repent, will your God cancel the judgment against Nineveh?"

"Dear lady," said Jonah, "he did not say such a thing. However, he is *'a gracious and compassionate God, slow to anger and abounding in love, a God who relents from sending calamity'"* (Jonah 4:2).

Jonah added, "Maybe if the Ninevites lift their voices to him with contrite hearts, he will hear from heaven and cancel the judgment. But I cannot declare as his word any more or less than what he told me to say."

"Do you have a place to stay while you are in Nineveh?" asked Adorina.

"No, dear lady," replied Jonah. "At night, I sleep outdoors by the cool waters of the River Khosr."

"That is splendid," said Adorina. "I have trustworthy friends who own a small house by the river's edge. I want to shelter you in their house. Do you accept?"

"Thank you, dear lady; I accept," said Jonah. "The Lord bless you for your kindness and the Lord bless your trustworthy friends for their kindness."

Unknown to Adorina and Jonah, the watchful eyes of Aho, Gewargis, and Nuhro were upon them. "Is that not the governor's daughter?" asked Aho. "We must tell Malkuno she is conspiring with the Hebrew. Anyway, we will continue to follow him at a distance."

𒅓 𒂅𒀉 𒅓𒌋

Adorina heard hateful voices against Jonah among some of the Ninevites. Concerned his life may be in danger, she went to Rabbu, explained things, and sought his help. Rabbu says, "Although I am not of the same religion as the Hebrew, I abhor murder. I will help you protect him. I suppose you must keep this matter from your father. I am sure he opposes the Hebrew and does not want you involved with him."

"That is so," said Adorina. "I arranged for some friends to shelter Jonah at their small house by the River Khosr."

"We can get Tamraz to help," said Rabbu. "He would be willing to get involved just for the thrill of a fight."

That night, Jonah went to the house at the river's edge to eat and rest. Rabbu and Tamraz followed him from a distance to watch over him. They noticed three strangers who seemed to be following Jonah. "See those three?" asked Tamraz. "They have been following Jonah for some time. Could they be assassins?"

"I think they are," said Rabbu. "Let us get closer."

Jonah was not aware that Aho, Gewargis, and Nuhro followed him to the house. He stepped out of the house to fill a jug with water. Aho says, "Here is our chance. We will kill him at the river's edge and dump his body in the water."

Then the three fell upon Jonah and beat him. "Prepare to die, Hebrew scum!" yelled Aho. The three expected Jonah to cower in fear, but he did not. "What is it with you, you worm of a wretched race?" yelled Aho. "Do you not fear death?"

Jonah replies, "When a man is thrown into a stormy sea and almost drowns, is swallowed by a huge fish, is forced to spend three days and three nights in its belly, and then is vomited out, not much remains that can frighten him."

"So, you think we cannot frighten you, you pile of pig dung!" yelled Aho. "Be frightened by this!" The assassins drew their daggers to give the prophet a thousand cuts. Then Tamraz fell upon them.

Nuhro yells, "A giant! Run for your lives!" and flees. Then Aho and Gewargis turned on Tamraz. But the mighty Tamraz grabbed both by their tunics, lifted them high above the ground, and banged their heads together so hard that their skulls were crushed. Then he tossed both bodies into the river. Thus ended the ill-fated attempt on Jonah's life.

The next day, Rabbu and Tamraz told Adorina about the night's scuffle. "My deepest gratitude to both of you," said Adorina. "And believe me, Jonah is most grateful too. But there may be more attempts on his life. We must remain vigilant."

Rabbu says, "We have friends you can hire to guard Jonah day and night. We served together in the army. They are good fighters who can take on any ruffians. Both Tamraz and I attest to their trustworthiness."

"Yes, introduce them to me," said Adorina. "I can hire some men to guard the house by the River Khosr along with some men to keep watch over Jonah as he walks through the city."

That same day, Malkuno learned his plan failed. He threw a rage, howling like a demon. "That treacherous daughter of the governor wrecked our plan. It looks like she enticed her lowly admirer Rabbu and that giant peasant Tamraz to help her. We must move up our plan to seize power. It is time to incite a city riot."

Malkuno and his cult followers devised a violent scheme to seize control of Nineveh. "Tomorrow we strike. Woe to all who oppose us. You are dismissed."

𒐊 𒂍𒁉 𒐊𒌋

The next day, there is great turmoil in the streets of Nineveh. Malkuno, the priests of Ishtar, the temple guards, and a large loyal mob of armed ruffians began to sweep through the city wall-to-wall, demanding that mothers surrender their children to the temple of Ishtar. One mother tried to flee from the mob with her baby girl in her arms, but the ruffians cornered her and brought her before Malkuno.

"Lowly woman, we came for your child, and we will have her," said Malkuno. "The Queen of Heaven craves for her blood."

"No, do not take her; I beg you!" cried the mother.

"Hand over your child or die," said Malkuno. But she refused to hand over her child. "Slit her throat!" ordered Malkuno. A ruffian drew a dagger and slit her throat as ordered. Then a priest seized the baby girl and put her in a wagon bound for the temple of Ishtar.

Many onlookers were horrified. But one fellow said, "All glory to Ishtar, the great Queen of Heaven. Shame and death to any mother who refuses to hand over her child."

At one encounter, Adorina happened to be in the mob's path. She saw a woman running from the mob with her two baby boys in her arms. The mob caught up with her. "Do not take my babies!" she pleaded.

Then Malkuno appeared and said, "We take who we want, when we want, to where we want. Do not resist, lowborn woman."

"No, I beg you," she pleaded. "These innocent ones are my youngest. Please spare them, high priest."

"So you have more children?" asked Malkuno. "I have good news for you."

"Then you will spare my babies, high priest?" she asked.

"No," he said. "After we seize your two babies, you will have fewer mouths to feed. Is that not great news?" Malkuno laughed. "You should look at the bright side and thank me." Malkuno laughed again.

Then a priest of Ishtar tried to grab the two babies, but the mother resisted. Adorina was indignant. She picked up a large stone, took careful aim, and hurled it at the priest. It struck his head and he fell.

"Run!" cried Adorina.

"Thank you, dear lady!" cried the mother. Then she fled with her babies in her arms.

Malkuno said, "That is Nabukinuzur's daughter. Seize her! Take her alive! We will sacrifice her to Ishtar, and a most fitting sacrifice will she be."

A squad of temple guards fell upon Adorina, shackled her, and put her in the wagon bound for the temple of Ishtar. "People of Nineveh, we are coming for your children!" yelled Malkuno. "Do you hear me! We are coming for your children!"

Similar atrocities occurred as the mob moved from one end of the city to the other. Word of the mob violence reached the governor's ears. "This time Malkuno has gone way too far," said Nabukinuzur. "He must be stopped immediately! Palakh, my most trusted servant, take fast horses and chariot and ride to the city garrison. Tell the commander that the garrison is ordered to put down Malkuno's mob and rescue seized children. I give permission for the garrison to assault the temple of Ishtar."

Palakh says, "May I respectfully remind you, Governor, that the city garrison is diminished. The great and honorable King Ashurdan deployed most of the garrison to suppress violence in other parts of the land. The few men who remain are provincial troops. They are older men, not as battle-ready as our regular soldiers."

"They will have to do," said Nabukinuzur. "Depart at once, Palakh."

"As you command, Governor," said Palakh.

Meanwhile, Rabbu and Tamraz heard about the commotion while going about their usual business in the main square. "Malkuno deserves a thousand deaths," said Tamraz.

"I agree," said Rabbu. "The provincial troops should be able to quench his mob."

Then Saliba, a close army friend of Rabbu and Tamraz, ran up to them and said, "Have you heard what they did to Adorina? Malkuno seized her and carried her off to the temple of Ishtar to be sacrificed."

Rabbu cried out in agony.

"Are you sure of this?" asked Tamraz.

Saliba replied, "There are eyewitness reports. Several people recognized Adorina. She risked her life to save a mother and her two babies."

"Does the governor know about this?" asked Rabbu, struggling to get coherent words out of his mouth.

Saliba replied, "A messenger was sent to him with word of Adorina's snatching along with a request to deploy the local garrison against the mob. But given the distances and travel times involved, the troops might not arrive in time."

Rabbu said, "Tamraz, we must assemble a host at once and head for the temple of Ishtar to rescue Adorina and the other victims of Malkuno's treachery. We cannot wait for the provincial troops. They might arrive too late."

"Rabbu, we go to war once more," said Tamraz. "I thirst for a good fight! Between your sword and my spears, we will send Malkuno and his underlings to the bottomless pit. It will be like old times. Saliba, will you join us?"

"I will," said Saliba, "and so will thirty of my battle-hardened army friends with fast horses. They carry swords, axes, spears, and maces. Several saw their own children carried off. They are eager to assault the temple of Ishtar to rescue their children. I, for one, cannot wait for a chance to bury my axe in Malkuno's evil heart."

"I can bring about twenty of my battle-hardened army friends," said Tamraz. "Most are spearmen, archers, and slingers, but they do not have horses, which are hard to come by these days."

"Not to worry," said Saliba. "We will ride double. It is still faster than going on foot. Rabbu, ride with me. You and I will discuss our strategy on the way."

"Then we ride as a battle-hardened host of about fifty," said Rabbu. "Though our host be small, we are strong, daring, and lion brave. We will subdue the temple guards and priests and rescue Adorina and the children. And we will slay that monster Malkuno."

"We be lion brave once more!" said Tamraz.

"Let us gather the men, horses, and arms without delay," said Saliba. "Time is short."

𒀭 𒂗𒇷 𒀭𒌋

The host of about fifty men made haste to the precinct of Ishtar at Kuyunjik. Rabbu and Saliba rode together. "Saliba, what is the best way to assault the temple?" asked Rabbu.

"We must storm the inner sanctum as quickly as possible," said Saliba. "That is where Malkuno and his minions will be sacrificing victims. The fastest way is a direct assault at the southwest gate. From there, we cross a small outer courtyard, then we pass through a gate that opens to a large inner courtyard. The entrance to the anteroom is at the far end of the inner courtyard. The entrance to the inner sanctum is at the back of the anteroom."

"We will be out in the open until we are inside the anteroom," said Rabbu. "If Malkuno has archers or slingers, we could be vulnerable. Are you sure this is the best way?"

"It is the fastest way," replied Saliba. "We can attack at other gates, but we may have to charge uphill. The terrain near the southwest gate is flat."

"Then the southwest gate it is, Saliba," said Rabbu. "Are you sure of the temple layout?"

"Most certainly," replied Saliba. "A friend used to work there as a painter. He explained the layout to me. It has not changed much since the days of King Shamshi Adad or King Tukulti Ninurta."

"I am counting on the element of surprise," said Rabbu. "The provincial troops should be engaging Malkuno's mob by now. He will not be expecting a direct assault on the temple."

The host arrived at the southwest gate of the precinct of Ishtar. "There is smoke rising from the sanctuary," said Saliba. "That means the sacrificial fire is lit. We may be too late to rescue some of the victims."

"We will save as many as we can," said Rabbu. The host overpowered the guards and poured through the gate.

"Men, move quickly through the courtyard to the next gate," shouted Saliba. The host ran across the courtyard without opposition, reached the next gate, stormed it with ease, and ran across the inner courtyard toward the anteroom. They cut down the few guards at the entrance to the anteroom and then poured inside.

"Leave some men in this room to ensure we are not ambushed from the rear," said Rabbu to Saliba. "The rest of you, follow me!"

Rabbu, Tamraz, Saliba, and their companions burst into the inner sanctum of the sacred precinct of Ishtar. The men shuddered as they beheld the horrifying sight. The sanctum's appearance is macabre and gloomy. It is wide and long. Its walls rise high above the precinct. The altar of Ishtar stands on an elevated stone platform at the far-left end of the room. It has a large gaping pit of fire bordered by a row of stones. A colossal statue of the Queen of Heaven stands behind the fiery pit. An elaborate stone stairway leads up to the altar. A large cage along a wall is filled with live children to be sacrificed. They are crying and screaming in terror. The walls have rows of grotesque idols and other heathen images. "This is a scene from the pit of hell," said Saliba.

Rabbu sees a huge Nubian priest with the face of a squid dragging Adorina up the stairs to drop her alive into the fiery pit. Adorina struggled to free herself, but the Nubian struck her, and she screamed. The Nubian reached the top of the stairs. Rabbu saw he could not reach Adorina in time to save her, so he cried out, "Tamraz, see the Nubian carrying Adorina to the altar! Run him through with a spear, taking great care to miss Adorina!"

"My spear will drink the blood of that Nubian!" shouted Tamraz. He drew a spear, took perfect aim, as he did before in a dozen fierce battles, and hurled it at the Nubian. The spear ran the Nubian through without touching Adorina, and he fell. But when the Nubian fell, Adorina fell, rolled down the stairs, and struck her head against a stone post at the bottom. There she lay bleeding from a head wound. Rabbu cried out, "Adorina!" but heard no answer.

At that moment Malkuno appeared at the top of the stairs wielding his enormous broadsword; at least a hundred armed temple guards and priests stood behind him. Rabbu saw him and shouted, "Malkuno, you are brave and mighty against helpless women and children, but now you face a host of battle-hardened soldiers. This day, you and your lackeys will surely die!"

Malkuno shouted back, "You must be the lowly Rabbu! Do you really think you can take me? I am the greatest swordsman in all the land of Akkad! I will cleave you in two with my broadsword. Guards and priests, attack! Slay those brigands!" Most of Malkuno's men charged down the stairs while a few remained at the top to protect him.

Saliba took charge of the host. He shouted, "Men, fear not that we are outnumbered! Archers and slingers to the front! Shoot Malkuno's men to thin their ranks!" The archers and slingers went forward and began shooting arrows and hurling lethal round stones at Malkuno's men. Many of his men fell as arrows pierced their hearts and stones smashed their skulls. Saliba shouted, "Spearmen to the front! Take aim and cast your spears!" The spearmen went forward, took aim, and cast their spears.

Tamraz drew another spear and hurled it at Malkuno's men with such strength and precision that it impaled three of them like balls of meat on a skewer. A squad of Malkuno's men raced toward Tamraz, five abreast, with spears extended. Tamraz swung his shield, shattered all five spears, and the squad fled in terror.

Seeing that Tamraz no longer had a weapon in hand, two guards tried to take him down with spears. But Tamraz grabbed both spears and pushed the guards back, impaling them on the extended spears of Malkuno's men behind them.

Another guard charged recklessly toward Tamraz with spear extended. Tamraz grabbed the spear with both arms and pole-vaulted the guard over his head. Then he hurled the spear against another guard and ran him through. The ranks of Malkuno's men dwindled more as they were run through by spears.

Saliba shouted, "Axe men to the front! Attack!" Saliba and his axe men went forward. With each swing of his axe, Saliba struck down a foe. His axe men were equally lethal against their opponents, lopping off limbs and heads, and burying axe blades in their opponents' hearts.

Saliba shouted, "Mace men to the front! Attack!" The mace men went forward and fell upon Malkuno's men, crushing their skulls with each stroke. The carnage was great as Malkuno's men fell in large numbers. Though numerically superior, his temple guards and priests were no match for the battle-hardened host.

Rabbu shouted, "Swordsmen, follow me! We fight our way to the top of the platform to take down Malkuno!" Rabbu and Saliba's swordsmen fell upon the guards and priests and fought their way to the stairs. With each thrust of his sword, Rabbu slew another foe as he advanced toward the stairs followed by Saliba's swordsmen. They charged up the stairs, cutting down their foes in short order. Rabbu and a few of the men reached the top. Malkuno raised his mighty broadsword high over his head with both arms and swung at one of the men, cleaving him from the neck to the groin. Then he cleaved another and another. At the same time, Rabbu slew another guard or priest with each thrust of his sword.

Then Rabbu and Malkuno found themselves face-to-face. "Prepare to die, Rabbu, you brazen fool and hater of the great gods!" shouted Malkuno. "I will cleave you in two! Or better yet, I may let you live long enough for you to see your precious Adorina roast. I hope she survived her fall, so I can toss her into the fiery pit and enjoy hearing her scream while the flames lick her tender flesh."

Rabbu became enraged. Malkuno raised his mighty broadsword high over his head with both arms, preparing to swing at Rabbu. But in so raising his broadsword, he left his chest exposed. Rabbu lurched forward with sword extended and ran his sword through Malkuno's heart, grounding the handguard against Malkuno's chest as the blade extended out his back, drenched in blood and dripping.

"Your descent down the bottomless pit begins, Malkuno!" shouted Rabbu. Malkuno dropped his broadsword. With demonic strength he grabbed the hilt of Rabbu's sword with both hands and tried to pull it out. He managed to pull it out part way, then a little more, and a little more after that, spurting out blood with each pull. But as he pulled, he inadvertently backed up toward the row of stones bordering the fiery pit. Then his right heel struck a stone, he tripped over the row of stones, and fell headfirst into the gaping pit of fire. He let out such a scream of terror that it could be heard to the ends of the precinct. The flames consumed his flesh, and his body disintegrated into a billowing cloud of foul black smoke. Thus, the terrible Malkuno was no more.

When the temple guards and priests saw Malkuno's demise, they threw down their arms and surrendered. Saliba said to his men, "Back the prisoners against the wall, and keep them there until the provincial troops arrive."

"Let us slit their throats," said Tamraz.

"No, that would make us more like them," said Saliba. "Let the authorities decide their fate."

The prisoners pleaded to their captors. "Have mercy on us," cried one of the priests.

"We were only following orders," cried one of the temple guards.

Another guard cried, "We only did as we were told."

Rabbu was indignant. From the top of the stairs, he shouted, "What mercy did you show to the children who were to be thrown in the fire? What mercy did you show to the mothers your henchmen murdered? What mercy did you show to the governor's daughter? I tell you, you will receive no more mercy than you gave to your victims."

A priest said, "But Malkuno died in his own flames. Is that not enough to atone for the rest of us?"

Rabbu replied, "Nothing can atone for your high crimes."

At that moment, the room was filled with the trampling sound of rushing soldiers. The provincial troops had finally arrived. Their commander shouted, "Where is that beast Malkuno? We vanquished his mob, and now we have come for him and his lackeys! We know they are hiding in this temple."

"What remains of Malkuno is in the smoke of that gaping fiery pit," said Rabbu, pointing toward the altar. "Malkuno is no more."

"A fitting manner of death for that monster," said the commander. "Now, who are you, and who are these men with you?"

"I am Rabbu, and my companions and I are battle-hardened soldiers who served in the king's army," replied Rabbu. "We stormed the temple to rescue the governor's daughter and the children."

"You must give the governor an account of what happened here today," said the commander. "He stands at the sanctum entrance, anxiously awaiting news about his daughter. Has anyone seen her?"

Rabbu ran down the stairs and stepped over to Adorina, embraced her, and tearfully replied, "She fell and struck her head against a stone post. She is dying. Her body is already cold to the touch."

The commander faced the temple guards and priests and said, "You are all complicit in Adorina's death, in addition to your other high crimes, such as inciting mob violence, and kidnapping children for sacrifice with no law to justify your actions. Each of you deserves a thousand deaths."

"But sir, we were only following orders," repeated one of the temple guards. "It is all Malkuno's doing."

The commander said, "So you were just following orders? That is an old and worthless excuse. Nothing you say or do will save you now. Men, draw your swords and fall upon the guards and priests. Utterly destroy them! Spare no one!"

The temple guards and priests were terrified by the loud swishing sound of dozens of provincial troops simultaneously unsheathing their swords. Then the troops fell upon the guards and priests, hacking, slashing, and thrusting—then thrusting, slashing, and hacking more until all that remained of the guards and priests was a pile of decapitated bodies, severed heads, and entrails on the blood-drenched floor. Thus, the temple guards and priests of Ishtar were no more.

"Release the caged children," ordered the commander. "Find out who their parents are and make every effort to return them safely to their homes." The children heard and cheered. Some of Saliba's men rejoiced when they found their sons and daughters still alive in the temple. But some received terrible news and lamented deeply. "Men, gently pick up Adorina's body and take her to the governor," said the commander. "Rabbu, come with me."

Nabukinuzur cried in agony when he saw the troops carrying Adorina's body. He had not felt such pain since the day he lost his wife in a terrible accident. "How could the great gods have allowed this?" he sobbed.

Then Rabbu spoke to Nabukinuzur. "Governor, Adorina once spoke of an old man who lives in a tiny village a short distance from the main city gate. He is known for healing travelers injured by bandits or mauled by wild beasts. Please let me take Adorina to him. I will implore him to call on his god to heal her."

Nabukinuzur was bewildered. One of his aides said, "Governor, that old man might be practicing sorcery. It is not wise to trust him with your daughter. The great gods have taken her. It is their will. Let it be."

Nabukinuzur said, "At times like this, I wonder whether it is the will of the gods or the will of evil men unrestrained by uncaring gods. Either way, I see the gods as being capricious, cruel, and unjust. I cannot let it be. I must try to save Adorina. Rabbu, let us go together to the healer."

"But governor," said the aide, "because of your deep suffering, your state of mind is not right. Think about this and pray for peace and comfort from our great gods. With respect, sir, reconsider your decision to see that healer."

"Do not tell me what my state of mind is!" exclaimed Nabukinuzur. "It is *your* state of mind that is wrong, along with those who blindly follow the ways of our priests. We saw this day what the great gods brought about in Nineveh, and I say our great gods are not so great."

"You speak blasphemy, Governor!" exclaimed the aide. "Retract your words before the great gods decide to rain punishment on us."

Nabukinuzur said, "I spoke the truth, so I retract nothing. I will waste no more time listening to your nonsense. Now get out of my sight. Rabbu, we go to see the healer."

The commander said, "Governor, let me assign a squad of soldiers to accompany you to the healer."

"You may do so," said Nabukinuzur.

The commander turned to one of his officers and said, "Assemble a squad of six men and escort the governor, his daughter, and Rabbu wherever they go. Do not let them out of your sight."

"Yes sir," replied the officer.

The commander noticed Tamraz's huge size and said to him, "You look familiar. Did we serve together in the king's army?"

Tamraz replied, "Yes sir, I remember you. You commanded the regiment that defeated the Hittites in the north country. I am Tamraz."

"I remember you now, soldier," said the commander. "You were the finest spearman in the regiment. They called you 'strong dog.' I can almost say without exaggeration that each time you threw a spear, an entire row of Hittite soldiers fell. Come to think of it, I remember Rabbu now. He served in my regiment too. They called him 'mighty one.' I am honored to have served with both of you in the king's army."

"Rabbu and I were honored to serve under your command," said Tamraz. "Those were glory days."

"Those were my younger days, Tamraz," said the commander. "As you can see, we provincial troops are older warriors assigned to somewhat softer duties. But we did vanquish Malkuno's mob as we fought our way to the temple."

"Then your old men rose to the challenge and performed well," said Tamraz. "Who can ask for more?"

"I suppose you are right," said the commander. "We came through as we did in the war against the Hittites. We were lion brave once more."

"Rabbu and I have been close friends since that war," said Tamraz.

"Then you may accompany the governor, Rabbu, and the squad as they take Adorina to the healer," said the commander.

Rabbu said to Nabukinuzur, "Let me help you carry Adorina."

"No," replied Nabukinuzur. "I must carry her myself." Nabukinuzur picked up Adorina and departed in haste with Rabbu, Tamraz, and the squad.

They arrived at the old man's village. They found him at his usual spot, seated on a rock in front of the village. The old man looked directly at Rabbu and said, "I know why you have come. The Most High has seen the righteous works of the lady. He will heal her. Bring the lady to my house."

The entourage followed the old man to a humble house at the edge of the village. "Place the lady on the cot in the room on the right," he said. Nabukinuzur did as the old man said. "Rabbu, you may remain in the room and hold the lady's hand if you wish," said the old man. "The rest of you must wait outside the room. Governor, with respect, you must wait outside too." The old man entered the room, closed a curtain behind him, and began to pray in his native tongue.

The entourage heard everything on the other side of the curtain. Nabukinuzur meditated in silence.

"What tongue is that?" asked Tamraz.

"I am not sure, but I think it is the native tongue of the Hebrews," replied the squad leader.

A trooper in the squad laughed and said, "It sounds like gibberish to me."

"Be quiet, bonehead!" said the squad leader. "Show some respect and serenity."

"Yes sir!" replied the trooper.

Rabbu gazed adoringly at Adorina even as she lay dead on the cot. She was still so beautiful. He caressed her. Tears flowed from his eyes as he held her cold hand. But as the old man continued to pray, Adorina's head wound disappeared slowly. Even the bloodstains on her clothing disappeared. Her hand started to feel warm to the touch. Rabbu kissed her lips, and they felt warm. Her arm started to feel warm. Rabbu could feel her pulse. Then she opened her eyes, looked at Rabbu, and smiled. Rabbu put his arms around her.

"Rabbu, my beloved," she said, "I knew you would come for me and the children." Rabbu felt dizzy, like his head was spinning. His heart melted. He started to lift Adorina from the cot, but she stood up in her own strength. The men at the other side of the curtain heard everything and were astonished.

The old man opened the curtain and said, "Give glory to the Most High. The lady was not dead. She was just asleep. Come in and see." Nabukinuzur and Tamraz ran into the room and saw Adorina alive, standing, and smiling, with Rabbu joyfully holding her hand. They saw that the wound on her head was gone. Even the bloodstains on her clothing were gone. Nabukinuzur embraced Adorina. The old man, Rabbu, Adorina, Tamraz, and Nabukinuzur stepped out of the room. All the men rejoiced when they saw Adorina alive. Then they all bowed to the old man as to a god, utterly amazed and awestruck. But the old man said, "Do not bow to me. I am just a man like you. I am but a humble servant of the Most High. Bow down to him and to him alone!"

Nabukinuzur asked Adorina, "Daughter, did you have any visions while you were asleep?"

"Yes," she replied. "I saw what appeared to be a throne room. Seated on the throne was one whose face was brighter than the sun. I saw amazing winged creatures of pure light. I think the Hebrews call them angels. I heard beautiful music. The place was so peaceful and majestic. I did not want to leave, but I knew it was not my time to go into eternity."

"Did the old man's god speak to you?" asked Nabukinuzur.

She replied, "Yes, I heard him, not with sound, but with thoughts in my mind. I remember them. He said he comes to our land with healing in his wings. I did not fully understand what he meant. And then I woke up in this house."

Nabukinuzur turned to the old man and said, "Sir, please tell me your name that I may honor it along with the name of your god."

The old man replied, "Just remember me as one who walks in the spirit of Elijah, and the God you have chosen to honor is the God of Abraham, Isaac, and Israel."

"The God of the Hebrews?" asked Nabukinuzur in amazement.

"Yes," replied the old man, "the Most High, the Ancient of Days, Jehovah Rapha. He healed your daughter. Give glory to him."

Rabbu faced the old man and said, "Truly, the God you serve is worthy. I renounce the gods of the Babylonians, the Assyrians, the Chaldeans, and the Akkadians. I now pledge my life in service to your God."

"The Most High accepts your pledge," said the old man. "Now let us serve the lady food and drink as she recovers from her harrowing experience."

𒅍 𒂖 𒅍𒌋

The next day, Rabbu, Tamraz, Saliba, and their companions stood before Nabukinuzur in his judgment hall and gave an account of their actions at the temple of Ishtar. The great ones were assembled before the governor. Adorina stood at her father's side.

"You performed a great deed for our city and our nation," said Nabukinuzur. "Even amid the trials our country is going through, there was much rejoicing as the children were returned to their parents. And of course, news of the demise of Malkuno and his cult followers was received jubilantly by most of the people. But now I have two other matters to address. Rabbu, I know you have eyes for Adorina, and I want to reward you for saving her life. But we have marriage laws that we must comply with. After all, the rule of law is what keeps us together as a civilized country. You are a commoner, and she is of noble birth. Our laws do not allow union of a commoner with a noble person."

Then Palakh, Nabukinuzur's most trusted servant, whispered in the governor's ear. No one else in the hall heard what he told the governor. Nabukinuzur said, "My most trusted servant just reminded me that as high official of our great city, I have authority to confer honors and rank upon citizens who excel at great deeds. Rabbu, Tamraz, Saliba, and companions, for your valiant exploits in defeating the recent menace to our city and for rescuing the innocent from death, it is my privilege to confer on you rank of nobility. That means Rabbu may lawfully wed my daughter."

At that, Rabbu and Adorina ran toward each other, embraced, and kissed. Rabbu's heart melted as he put his arms around Adorina. As usual, when he is with Adorina, he feels dizzy as if his head is spinning.

"Adorina, my beloved," said Rabbu, "will you stay with me and be my bride?"

"Yes I will, Rabbu," she replied gently with a warm smile. Tamraz, Saliba, and the companions cheered.

"I must now turn my attention to another pressing matter,"

said Nabukinuzur. "Rabbu, Tamraz, Saliba, and companions, you are dismissed. Great ones, remain for a while. We turn now to the matter of the Hebrew Jonah preaching doom for our city."

𒅎 𒂗 𒅎𒁹

That evening a messenger arrives and speaks to Nabukinuzur and his great ones. "Governor and great ones, I bring news regarding the people's response to the Hebrew. Many believe his message, especially in the aftermath of Malkuno's fall and the destruction of his cult. Moreover, many remain concerned over the total solar eclipse that occurred in the year of Esdu-Sarabe. It most certainly is an omen that Nineveh is doomed. The people are in fear. The whole nation has endured seven years of tribulation, with plagues, war, and rumors of war. There is no end in sight. Governor and great ones, considering all these things, the people are convinced the great gods are either impotent or have forsaken us. They are turning to the Hebrew god for deliverance. They gather in groups throughout the city to pray. Here and there some groups gather by the dozens, some groups gather by the hundreds, and some groups gather by the thousands. I would say twenty thousand have gathered by now, maybe more. The number grows by the hour. There are also many reports of people fasting, putting on sackcloth, and mourning. Some even put sackcloth on their animals and made them partakers of mourning, as in the way of the Persians. Governor and great ones, the people expect to hear reassuring voices from the governing authorities. What shall we tell them?"

Seeing it was getting late, Nabukinuzur said, "We shall retire for the evening and take up these crucial matters again tomorrow morning. You are all dismissed."

That night, Nabukinuzur had a ghastly dream. He saw a

terrifying vision of Nineveh being destroyed by sword and fire. It was as if the armies of all the nations of the world joined forces, laid siege to the great city, breached its walls, and poured into the city, killing every man, woman, and child in sight. There was great slaughter everywhere. Then they put the entire city to the torch. Everything burned to the ground. Not one building remained standing. Nabukinuzur woke up sweating. He ordered a servant to find an interpreter of dreams, but no interpreter was found who could comfort him.

CHAPTER 7

PEACE IN THE LAND

The next morning Nabukinuzur addresses the assembly of great ones. "My esteemed great ones, allow me to describe a ghastly dream I had last night. I saw a terrifying vision of Nineveh being destroyed by sword and fire. It was as if the armies of all the nations of the world joined forces, laid siege to the great city, breached its walls, and poured into the city, killing every man, woman, and child in sight. There was great slaughter everywhere. Then they put the entire city to the torch. Everything burned to the ground. Not one building remained standing. Then I woke up sweating. I am convinced the dream is a warning. We have endured seven years of tribulation. These have been years like no other, and they are not over yet. I need not remind you that our situation is bleak. Our great gods failed us. A circle of unending violence is closing around Nineveh. I am convinced the Hebrew God is coming against us with wrath and fury. Even so, I know he is a God of mercy and a worker of miracles. My daughter's mortal head wound was healed by the power of the Hebrew God. I am convinced he can heal our land and might do so if we turn to him with contrite hearts. But we must face the grim possibility that

Nineveh will fall if he does not deliver us. If so, just when will the end come, and what can we do to prepare? Should we evacuate the entire city and return in better times? How can we appease the wrath of the Hebrew God? How much time do we have? Speak your minds with candor."

Then Eshai spoke. "Governor and fellow great ones, to unravel the mystery of the timing of the calamity to come, we must understand the sacred writings of our religion and the Hebrew religion. Our Enuma Elish, which we inherited from Babylonia in days of old, records the creation of the world and man in seven tablets. Similarly, the sacred Hebrew writings record the creation of the world and man in seven days. It is no coincidence that both writings culminate in seven somethings, whether they are seven tablets or seven days. I believe we are in a period of seven somethings, and each something is a year of tribulation. I believe the final doom will come at the end of these seven years. I would start counting the seven years with the very day that pestilence first broke out in our land. The Hebrew declared that in forty days our great city would be overthrown. Consider the first day he preached, add forty days, and you arrive at the seventh anniversary of the first outbreak of plague. On that precise day, Nineveh will fall. Woe to Nineveh!"

Then Gabbara spoke. "Governor and fellow great ones, it is written in the sacred Hebrew texts that in days of old, their God destroyed the infamous cities of Sodom and Gomorrah at sunrise. I presume the Hebrew God will use similar timing with us. Therefore, expect the doom of Nineveh to occur at sunrise on the seventh anniversary of the first outbreak of plague, the very day just spoken of by Eshai."

Then Bartulme spoke. "Governor and fellow great ones, why are you so sure it is the Hebrew god who comes against us? Why give glory to their god of goats, camels, and slaves? Do you not remember that in days of old, the great fish-god Oannes warned he would arise from the sea to punish us for doing evil? Did our ancient writings not say that Oannes sends messengers from the sea? Did the Hebrew not cross the sea on his way to our land? I believe the Hebrew is not a prophet of the Hebrew god, but a messenger of Oannes. It is to the great Oannes to whom we must turn and beg for mercy."

Then Muska spoke. "Governor and fellow great ones, we need not fear the Hebrew god. Do not forget our army defeated Israel's King Ahab and his eleven allies at the great battle of Karkar about a hundred years ago. After their defeat, the Israelites were forced to bring annual tribute to Assyria. You have all seen the obelisk of our great and honorable King Shalmaneser in Nimrud. Do you not recall the image of the Israelite King Jehu humbling himself before our king when he delivered tribute? If the Hebrew god is so mighty, why would he let the kings of Israel suffer defeat and humiliation? I say we need not fear Israel's god of goats, camels, and slaves. We must be more faithful to our own great gods. If we sacrifice to the gods with increased zeal and intensity, they will hear from their heavenly abodes and deliver us from this tribulation."

Then Elqosh spoke. "Governor and fellow great ones, let us not underestimate the power of the Hebrew God. It is said that he sent ten plagues to Egypt to coerce Pharaoh to release the Hebrew slaves in the days of the one known as Moses. Each plague dethroned a god of Egypt. It is also written that he destroyed the army of Egypt in the Red Sea when Pharaoh sent it in pursuit of the slaves. Moreover, the Hebrew God delivered lightning victories to the Israelite commander Joshua at the battles of Jericho, Hazor, and others. Why, even the awesome idol of Baal in the city of Hazor could not deliver that city from the fury of the Hebrew God. And let us remember that in the days of the Hebrew kings David and Solomon, the Hebrew God delivered stunning victories to his chosen people in wars against the Philistines and other foes. But Moses, Joshua, David, and Solomon were faithful servants of their God; the Hebrew God only turns his face away when his people reject him. The Israelite King Ahab rejected his God, so Ahab's defeat was not due to weakness on the part of the Hebrew God. It was due to faithlessness on the part of Ahab, who turned to Baal. The Hebrew God is a god of wonders and miracles. I believe he will bless us if we turn away from our own idols and turn to him with open hearts."

Then Muska spoke again. "Governor and fellow great ones, what I just heard here is blasphemy against our great gods! Governor, that healing your daughter got from an old Hebrew was not a miracle. Undoubtedly it was accomplished by witchcraft. Your daughter and you fell for an act of sorcery. Moreover, it is people like Eshai, Gabbara, and Elqosh who arouse the anger of our great gods by appealing to puny foreign gods. Perhaps Eshai, Gabbara, Elqosh, and their supporters should be sacrificed! Your own daughter shares this guilt. She should be sacrificed too, and almost was."

"Enough, Muska!" exclaimed Nabukinuzur. "I will not tolerate insults and slander among our great ones, and I most certainly will not tolerate insulting words against my own daughter! Does anyone have more to say?"

Then Gabbara spoke again. "Governor and fellow great ones, I now remember something else from the sacred Hebrew writings. They say the Hebrew God promised to Abraham, the ancient Hebrew patriarch, that for the sake of ten righteous ones, he would spare all the inhabitants of the infamous cities of Sodom and Gomorrah. Do you realize the implications of that? If the Hebrew God was willing to spare all of Sodom and Gomorrah for the sake of only ten, would he not also be willing to spare our entire great city if thousands of our subjects repent and cry out to him with contrite hearts? That may be the very reason their God gave us a warning in time, to give the people space to repent. If Eshai's understanding of the chronology of events to come is correct, then we have only ten days remaining to repent. The end draws near. Governor, you must issue, without delay, a decree of repentance to the people of Nineveh. If we repent in the precious little time that remains, the Hebrew God might hear from heaven and spare our great city. Perhaps he may even deliver all of Assyria from tribulation. But if we are to repent on behalf of our entire nation, repentance of hundreds, thousands, or even ten thousand might not be enough. It must be mass repentance of Nineveh from end to end, even a hundred thousand, from the highest to the lowest of our subjects. You must make it clear that only mass repentance may suffice. Governor, command the people of Nineveh to repent from one end of the city to the other."

"I lack authority to issue a decree of mass repentance without the king's approval," said Nabukinuzur. "After all, even as governor and high official, I am just a viceroy."

Then Goriel spoke. "Governor and fellow great ones, it seems we have a divided opinion here. But I am convinced by the wise words of Eshai, Gabbara, and Elqosh. In the past seven years, we saw how our great gods were dethroned by the Hebrew God, not unlike the way he dethroned the gods of Egypt in the days of Moses. It is said that his tenth and final plague was the slaughter of the firstborn of Egypt from the highest to the lowest of the Egyptians. Let us seek in earnest the Hebrew God and perhaps spare our great city from the same fate as the firstborn of Egypt."

Then Adorina stood up and spoke. "Governor and great ones, some of you may think it is not my place to address this assembly, but I cannot remain silent. I am compelled to speak. As you already know, I met Jonah and spoke with him several times. I find him to be a man of integrity. I believe he speaks the truth, and I believe he is a faithful emissary of the God of Israel. Moreover, I know Jonah's God is a true God. By his power, I was healed of a mortal head wound. I saw the wonders of his heavenly abode in a vision. Know that Jonah was reluctant to come to our great city. He even tried to run from his God by boarding a ship bound for the far western end of the world. But his God sent a storm and cut the journey short. Jonah was thrown into the rough sea and was rescued by his God so he could accomplish his mission. Do you not see the obvious? This is not about us reaching up to the great gods of Assyria for deliverance. It is about the God of Israel reaching down to us through his servant Jonah. I believe the God of Israel has offered a hand of friendship to us, but only for a short time. I also believe that if we respond with contrite hearts, he will spare us from the final calamity to come. But if we mock him, we will most certainly be doomed on the very day and hour that Eshai and Gabbara spoke of. Moreover, look at the calendar and see that tomorrow is the first of the last ten days before the final calamity strikes. Let us not repeat the mistake of the great and honorable King Adadnirari, who some years ago commanded the nation to trust only the god Nabu and no other. While his intentions were honorable, he told the nation to surrender its fate to an idol that cannot see, hear, or speak. Father, I believe it was the very God that Jonah worships who sent that ghastly dream to you as a prophetic warning. Let us now trust in the living God, the God of Israel. I appeal to you as a loyal subject of Assyria and as your daughter to seek an immediate audience with the great and honorable King Ashurdan and adjure him to issue to our people a decree of mass repentance. The matter now rests on your shoulders as governor of Nineveh. It is up to you now to exhort our king to take action that may save Nineveh. The same God who sent Jonah to us has commissioned you as well. As goes Nineveh, so goes Assyria."

Then Nabukinuzur spoke again. "My dear daughter, you spoke with the wisdom of a sage! My esteemed great ones, I have decided on a course of action. I will bring Jonah before our king. I will have Jonah speak his prophecy as he stands face-to-face with the great and honorable Ashurdan. I am convinced that if Jonah's God truly is God, the king will hear Jonah and will be obliged to act. But if Jonah's God is not God, the king will either kill Jonah or run him out of the country. Palakh, my faithful servant, assemble a squad of soldiers and have them find Jonah. He is to be brought to me not as a prisoner, but as a free man. Do this at once."

"As you command, governor," said Palakh. He departed and did as the governor ordered.

Palakh returned within the hour and reported to Nabukinuzur. "Governor, the soldiers found the Hebrew Jonah while he was preaching to the people at the city square. As ordered, they brought him not as a prisoner, but as a free man. He is just outside the door under guard. Shall I bring him in?"

"Yes, do so at once," said Nabukinuzur.

Jonah was brought before Nabukinuzur, flanked by two soldiers. Nabukinuzur spoke to Jonah. "Jonah, servant of the Hebrew God, I do not fully understand what you are preaching. Yet I believe you have a message of the utmost importance to my people. I want you to stand before my king, and tell him this word you are preaching. If the power of your God really is behind your word, my king will hear and act accordingly. But if the power of your God is not behind your word, my king will declare you a false prophet and will have you run out of the country at best, or have you tortured and slain at worst. Do you have enough faith in your God to stand before my king and risk the fate I just explained to you?"

"I do," replied Jonah.

"Jonah," said Nabukinuzur, "I will not force you to do this. It must be of your own free will."

"I go before your king willingly," said Jonah.

"Very well," said Nabukinuzur. "I have a strange feeling that your fate and my fate are now intertwined. When we stand before the king, we will either stand together or fall together. Palakh, my faithful servant, summon Eshai, Gabbara, and Elqosh. Prepare a squad of chariots with drivers and fast horses. Assemble a squad of soldiers for escort. Do so at once."

"As you command," said Palakh.

A little while later, Palakh returned with Eshai, Gabbara, and Elqosh. Nabukinuzur spoke. "We will all ride to Nimrud with Jonah to see our king. Eshai, Gabbara, and Elqosh, I trust your understanding of the sacred Hebrew writings is deep enough that you may answer questions posed by our king. Palakh, when can we leave?"

"Whenever you say, Governor," he replied.

"Then we leave at once," said Nabukinuzur.

And so, the entourage departed to Nimrud. As they rode, Palakh instructed Jonah on how he is to address the king. "Jonah, my master Governor Nabukinuzur wants the great and honorable King Ashurdan to hear from your own lips your prophecy of doom for Nineveh. We will be escorted to the throne room of the king. You are to stop when we stop and bow when we bow. Remain silent until the king commands you to speak. And be sure the first words that come out of your mouth are 'great and honorable king.' When the king speaks to you, do not interrupt him. When he is satisfied he has heard enough from you, he will tell you so. Remain silent unless the king speaks to you again. Never forget you will be standing before the ruler of the four quarters of the world. Always show the utmost respect. Know that it may cost you your very head if you fail at this."

Jonah replied, "I will comply in all those matters."

Early the next morning, the entourage approached the citadel of Nimrud. They noticed a large host of infantry, cavalry, and chariots gathering just outside the walls.

"It looks like the king is preparing to launch a military expedition," said Palakh. "Why else would such a host be gathering here?"

"Probably an expedition to suppress some of the violence in the land," said Nabukinuzur. "I hear the violence in Gozan is particularly severe. Judging by the size of the host, I venture to say they are ready to depart at any time."

The entourage approached the east gate of the citadel of Nimrud. When they reached the gate, a soldier said, "Stop! All who seek entry into the king's citadel must declare their name and purpose of visit."

Nabukinuzur responded, "I am Nabukinuzur, governor and high official of the great city of Nineveh. I bring a message of utmost importance to the king and his great ones." The soldier commanded the entourage to wait. He sent a messenger to the guards of the northwest palace complex. After a minimal delay, the messenger reported back to the soldier.

The soldier said, "The great and honorable King Ashurdan will see you at the northwest palace. But there will be some delay while he tends to urgent matters of state. You are commanded to go to the main square of the citadel and wait there. When the king is ready to receive you, he will send a messenger and an escort to bring you to his throne room."

"As the king commands," replied Nabukinuzur. The entourage passed through the gate and made its way to the main square. They dismounted. Nabukinuzur said to Jonah, "Feel free to walk about the square but remain within sight at all times."

"I will comply," said Jonah.

Jonah wandered about the square while some soldiers watched him suspiciously. Several people strolling about the square noticed that he is a stranger. They talked about him among themselves.

"Who is that strangely dressed man?" asked a fellow.

"I am not sure," said another fellow. "I think he may be an Israelite."

"You mean someone from the land of Samaria?" asked another fellow. "What business has he in the king's citadel unless he is an ambassador?"

Another fellow said, "If he is an Israelite, he is also a Hebrew. The Hebrews are a strange people who worship a god of goats, camels, and slaves. Maybe he is here to beg favor from Assyria."

Another fellow said, "I heard about those Hebrews. They believe there is only one god. How silly of them! I suppose they do not have many holy days to celebrate if they have only one god."

Another fellow said, "I also heard the Hebrews are a mad race. Perhaps someday our king will send his army to Samaria to conquer and enslave their race."

Yet another fellow said, "No. They will drag us down if we add them to our empire. If there is a war, let the loser keep Israel. We can have the rest of the world." At that, they all laughed and went about their business.

Jonah noticed a huge dark obelisk as he strolled about the square. He approached it and examined it. It displayed images of dignitaries bringing tribute to the king of Assyria. It also had some inscriptions in a writing style that Jonah did not recognize. Then Jonah noticed an image that grieved his heart. It is the image of King Jehu of Israel bowing to King Shalmaneser of Assyria. *"How terrible to see one of our kings bow to the cruel and ruthless Shalmaneser of Assyria,"* thought Jonah. *"Shalmaneser inflicted great cruelties and tortures on the peoples he conquered, as did his father Ashurnasirpal. What a humiliation for Jehu and for Israel! This must go back to the follies of King Ahab, who yoked Israel to an alliance of several heathen nations against Assyria to quench Assyria's westward expansion. The alliance was defeated at the battle of Karkar. Ahab was humiliated, even though he marched to war with ten thousand soldiers and two thousand chariots. To this day, the king of Israel sends tribute to the king of Assyria as a form of extortion."* Jonah also noticed an image of a heathen king bowing to Shalmaneser. *"It looks like the heathen king is preparing to kiss Shalmaneser's feet, thus acknowledging him as his god,"* thought Jonah. *"But Jehu kept some distance between himself and Shalmaneser. He did not kiss his feet. Good for him. He maintained some dignity in the matter."*

Jonah also noticed several pairs of colossal lamassus as he strolled about the square. But this time, they did not seem to be staring at him. Their eyes did not seem to roll toward him as he moved about. Jonah thought, *"Lamassu, you no longer frighten me. I now call you 'lamassu falling.' For when Nineveh falls, you will fall with her. Who then will fear you?"*

Palakh asked Nabukinuzur, "Governor, are you going to tell the king about your daughter's miraculous healing of a mortal head wound?"

"I will bring that up as a final appeal only if the king obstinately refuses to heed Jonah's warning," replied Nabukinuzur. "But I believe Jonah's God can and will open the king's eyes to see the truth."

"A wise decision, Governor," said Palakh. "There is always the risk the king may respond like Muska. As you said the other day, Jonah's fate and your fate are now intertwined. You will both stand together before the king, or you will fall together."

"If I incur the king's wrath, I will take sole responsibility," said Nabukinuzur. "I will surrender alone to the king's judgment."

"Governor, allow me the privilege to stand with you regardless of the king's attitude toward you or toward Jonah," said Palakh.

"I respect and honor your loyalty, Palakh, my most trusted servant," said Nabukinuzur. "But above all, I hold dear your friendship. We will stand together in this." At that moment, a palace messenger arrived and commanded the entourage to proceed to the northwest palace complex.

A little while later, Nabukinuzur, Jonah, Palakh, Eshai, Gabbara, and Elqosh approached the king's throne. Assyrian custom does not allow foreigners like Jonah to stand close to the king, so the entourage stopped a few paces before the throne. All bowed before the king. "You may all rise," said Ashurdan. "My esteemed governor Nabukinuzur, know that I have an extremely urgent matter to attend to. Within the hour, I march to Gozan with an army to suppress the extreme violence over there. I am sure you noticed the host gathered just outside the walls. I was able to patch together an army by combining squads of soldiers from here and there that were not already committed to fighting violence in other parts of the land. They are not our best or most experienced soldiers, but they will have to do. I have little time to spare, but I can always make time for the governor of the great city. I just received word of the demise of Malkuno and his cult. I commend you for the way you disposed of that great criminal and his followers. You handled the matter superbly. Now, what business do you bring before me?"

"Great and honorable king, I bring before you Jonah, a Hebrew, who claims to be a prophet of his God," said Nabukinuzur. "He is preaching a word of doom for the great city. I want you to hear this word from his own lips. I confess I do not fully understand his message, yet I believe he is sincere, and that he speaks the word of the Hebrew God. Know that Jonah came here willingly, on pain of death if you judge him to be a false prophet."

Ashurdan said, "If he does not fear death for displeasing me, I at least owe him a chance to speak." Then he faced Jonah and said, "Hebrew, you may speak for yourself. What is this word you bring?"

At that moment, Jonah was filled with the spirit of the Most High. Any lingering fear departed from his heart. Not even the watchful eyes of the lamassus could disturb him now. He began to speak.

"Great and honorable king, I am Jonah, a Hebrew who worships the Lord, the God of Heaven, who made the sea and the dry land. I was sent by my Lord to deliver an urgent message to the people of the great city of Nineveh. At first, I was reluctant to obey my Lord. I fled to the port of Joppa and boarded a ship bound for the distant land of Tarshish, at the western end of the world. Along the way, a great wind came on the sea. It stirred a storm of such violence that the ship threatened to break up. In morbid fear, the sailors cried out to their gods for deliverance. They threw the cargo into the sea to lighten the ship, but to no avail. Then the sailors cast lots to find out who brought upon us the wrath of the gods, and the lot fell on me. I realized then that my running from my Lord brought this calamity upon the ship. I told the sailors to pick me up and throw me into the sea. I assured them my Lord would calm the sea if they did this. But the sailors did not heed my words at first. They tried their best to row back to land, but to no avail, as the sea turned even more violent. Alas, they picked me up and threw me overboard, and then the raging sea turned calm (Jonah 1:3–15). I descended into the depths of the Great Sea, expecting to drown as punishment for disobeying my Lord. But the Lord rescued me from the depths, for he sent a huge fish to swallow me. From inside the belly of the fish, I prayed to the Lord, and he answered me. For three days and three nights, the huge fish swam to the eastern shore of the Great Sea. Upon reaching the shore, the fish vomited me onto dry land at the command of the Lord. Then I made haste to the great city of Nineveh to proclaim this urgent message of utmost importance. Hear the word of the Lord. The wickedness of Nineveh has come up before him: 'Forty more days and Nineveh will be overthrown' (Jonah 3:4). Moreover, from the day I started to preach to the present, thirty-one days have passed; nine remain. In just nine more days, Nineveh will be overthrown."

Ashurdan laughed and said, "That is quite a fish story. If I had not found it amusing, I would have ordered your execution on the spot. Now tell me, Hebrew, just how is the doom of Nineveh to happen? Will a nation mightier than Assyria invade and destroy Nineveh? No such nation exists to the ends of the earth. Will the waters of the River Tigris rise and flood the great city? Will it be pestilence, famine, fire, or earthquake that consumes Nineveh? If you really do speak for a god, answer my questions."

Jonah replied, "Great and honorable king, as a prophet of God, I can only speak the words he gave me to speak. To speak more would be presumptuous. To speak less would be negligent. God has not told me everything. But he did warn that Nineveh will fall because of its wickedness."

Ashurdan said, "And what response does your god expect from us? Moreover, why should I fear the word of your god of goats, camels, and slaves? Did the armies of Assyria not already defeat Israel in battle? Did Assyria not force Israel to become another vassal state of our growing empire? Our gods of war are mightier than your god. We fear him not."

Jonah replied, "Great and honorable king, it is up to you how Assyria is to respond. Perhaps since the warning is in time, God is giving the people space to repent."

"What impudence!" cried one of Ashurdan's great ones. "Great and honorable king, must we indulge this blowhard any longer? I say have him bound, flogged, and thrown outside the citadel. Let the lions, hyaenas, and jackals of the land have him for fodder."

Ashurdan said, "Take the Hebrew to another room within the palace and keep him there until I decide his fate." Then two soldiers grabbed Jonah by his arms and dragged him to the grand hall at the right, passing between two enormous lamassus.

Jonah felt no fear when he saw the stony faces of the lamassus, and he felt no fear as he was dragged through their shadows. He thought, *"What is this? Revenge of the lamassus? No. Lamassu is falling. God will have his way. No fear!"*

Ashurdan spoke to Nabukinuzur. "I suppose you have good reasons to bring that Hebrew before me. If not, your days as governor may be cut short. Speak."

Then Nabukinuzur began to speak. "Great and honorable king, we have endured seven years of tribulation. We have suffered plague in the land and witnessed a grim portent in the heavens, followed by war, rumors of war, and more plague. In all our proud history, we have never seen days like these. Our great gods have not delivered us from the tribulation. Maybe it is time to hear and heed a message from another god. I cannot say with absolute certainty that Jonah speaks the word of a true God, but I cannot ignore what he says. If it were not for these seven years of tribulation, I would have dismissed Jonah's message. But I cannot ignore it, considering what is happening in our land. Already, thousands of your loyal subjects are turning to Jonah's God for deliverance. Many are praying, fasting, mourning, and putting on sackcloth. Some are putting sackcloth on their animals to make them partakers of mourning, as in the way of the Persians. You might not believe Jonah, but you cannot ignore him. Great and honorable king, there are only four possibilities. Jonah is either a lunatic, a liar, a buffoon, or a messenger of a true God. I implore you to decide here and now which of these four he is. If he is a lunatic, send him to the madman's prison. If he is a liar, cut out his lying tongue, bind him, and toss his body to the lions, hyaenas, and jackals outside the gates. If he is a buffoon, have him flogged and banished from the land forever on penalty of death. If he is a messenger of a true God, command the people to hear and heed his words. I can say no more."

Ashurdan stood and began to pace the room nervously. One of his eunuchs said, "Great and honorable king, surely, you are not impressed by the Hebrew's words. He speaks fantasy."

Another eunuch spoke. "Great and honorable king, surely, the Hebrew is insane. Heed not his words. Send him to the madman's prison."

Then a third eunuch spoke. "Great and honorable king, I believe Jonah. I believe his God sent him to us to speak a word that will alter the destiny of our great nation for years to come. The sacred Hebrew writings tell of an obscure and lowly Hebrew called Joseph. He was a prisoner in Egypt. The great pharaoh of Egypt had troubling dreams. No man was found who could interpret his dreams. Then Joseph was brought before Pharaoh, and he interpreted the dreams. He told Pharaoh famine was coming to the land. He told Pharaoh to fill the storehouses of Egypt with grain during plentiful times in preparation for lean times. Pharaoh did as Joseph said. When famine came, the storehouses of Egypt had enough food to feed the entire world. In those days, emissaries of our own country traveled to Egypt to buy grain for our people. Great and honorable king, I implore you to heed the words of Jonah with the same wisdom that Pharaoh heeded the words of Joseph. Just like Pharaoh responded wisely to a dream interpretation given to him by an obscure Hebrew prisoner, the king of Assyria should respond wisely to a message spoken to him by an obscure Hebrew prophet. That is my counsel to you, great and honorable king."

Ashurdan continued pacing. Then his heart softened. "Bring Jonah back in here," he said to the soldiers. They returned promptly with Jonah. Then Ashurdan faced Jonah and asked, "Jonah, did your God say that if we repent and turn from our ways, he will cancel the judgment against Nineveh?"

Jonah replied, "Great and honorable king, he did not say such a thing. However, he is *'a gracious and compassionate God, slow to anger and abounding in love, a God who relents from sending calamity'*" (Jonah 4:2). He added, "Maybe if the Ninevites lift their voices to him with contrite hearts, he will hear from heaven and cancel the judgment. But as I said before, I cannot declare as his word any more or less than what he told me to say."

Then Ashurdan faced Nabukinuzur and said, "Return at once to Nineveh with Jonah and the rest of your entourage. Issue in my name a decree to the people of Nineveh. Command them to put on sackcloth, pray, fast, and mourn for Nineveh. Even their animals must fast and mourn in sackcloth. Let everyone call urgently on Jonah's God as they pray. Let them give up their evil ways and their violence. Have them pray that Jonah's God may yet relent and with compassion turn from his fierce anger so that Nineveh will not perish (Jonah 3:7–9). As goes Nineveh, so goes Assyria."

At that moment, the senior military officer of Nimrud approached the throne and spoke to Ashurdan. "Great and honorable king," he said, "the donkeys that pull your chariot were unhitched and your war stallions were hitched to your chariot."

"Well," said Ashurdan, facing Nabukinuzur, "that is the sign the army is ready to march off to war. You have a decree to deliver, and I have an army to lead. I trust you to handle things properly, Nabukinuzur. Do not make me regret my decision. You are dismissed." At that, the entourage departed and returned to Nineveh in haste.

Early the next morning, Nabukinuzur called an emergency meeting of his great ones at the judgment hall of his palace in Nineveh. He summoned his scribe. The scribe arrived with servants carrying several wet clay tablets and styli for writing. They set up a table and arranged the tablets. "Scribe, record the following decree," said Nabukinuzur:

> *By the decree of the king and his* [great ones]: *Do not let people or animals, herds or flocks, taste anything; do not let them eat or drink. But let people and animals be covered with sackcloth. Let everyone call urgently on God. Let them give up their evil ways and their violence. Who knows? God may yet relent and with compassion turn from his fierce anger so that we will not perish.*
>
> —Jonah 3:7–9

Nabukinuzur continued, "Moreover, by the decree of the governor of Nineveh and his great ones, the Hebrew visitor called Jonah is not to be harmed. Anyone who lays hands on him will be put to death without pity. Jonah is free to roam about Nineveh and speak the word of God without hindrance. Hear his words. If he commands you to do something, obey. You are free to offer him hospitality. I, Nabukinuzur, governor and high official of the great city of Nineveh, command this in the name of the great and honorable Ashurdan, strong king, king of Assyria, king of the world, king of the four quarters. So let it be written, and so let it be done. Scribe, prepare and distribute many copies of these decrees. Dispatch emissaries with orders to read them aloud to the ends of the city by day and by night." The scribe obeyed.

Nabukinuzur sat on his judgment chair. He commanded a servant to bring sackcloth and dust of the earth. The servant obeyed and returned promptly with the goods. Nabukinuzur commanded the servant to pour the dust of the earth on the floor of the judgment hall. Nabukinuzur rose from his judgment chair, took off his stately robes, covered himself with sackcloth, and sat down in the dust poured on the floor.

Then he said, "Even though I am governor and high official of our great city, I too must obey the decrees. My high rank does not make me so pompous and proud that I can disregard them. I sit here humbly on dust of the earth, covered in sackcloth. I will pray in silence to the true God. Who will join me?"

Adorina put on sackcloth, sat next to her father, and began to pray in silence. She did not disrobe. Even so, some lustful men in the judgment hall were hoping she would. Palakh joined the governor and his daughter. Then one by one the great ones joined the governor, Adorina, and Palakh, except Muska, who stormed out of the hall in anger.

Starting that very day, the word went forth far and wide throughout Nineveh. Each day, emissaries read aloud the decrees:

People of the great city of Nineveh, hear the word of the great and honorable King Ashurdan, strong king, king of Assyria, king of the world, king of the four quarters:

Do not let people or animals, herds or flocks, taste anything; do not let them eat or drink. But let people and animals be covered with sackcloth. Let everyone call urgently on God. Let them give up their evil ways and their violence. Who knows? God may yet relent and with compassion turn from his fierce anger so that we will not perish (Jonah 3:7–9).

Now hear the word of the noble Nabukinuzur, governor and high official of the great city of Nineveh: The Hebrew visitor called

Jonah is not to be harmed. Anyone who lays hands on him will be put to death without pity. Jonah is free to roam about Nineveh and speak the word of God without hindrance. Hear his words. If he commands you to do something, obey. You are free to offer him hospitality.

The decrees were read aloud at the city gates, along the city walls, at the river landings, at the four corners of the city, at the hills of Kuyunjik, along the banks of the Rivers Khosr and Tigris, at the marketplaces, at the main square, at the temples, at the soldiers' barracks, at the government centers, in the taverns, in the residential areas, and even inside brothels and prisons. The word was heard north to south, east to west, wall to wall. Wherever people gathered, the emissaries read aloud the decrees of the king and the governor.

The multitudes responded. Tens of thousands put on sackcloth and gathered all over the city to pray, fast, and call on the Most High with contrite hearts. Even the animals went without food or water. They bore sackcloth as partakers of mourning, as in the way of the Persians. The people stopped sacrificing to the gods of Assyria. No longer was the smoke of sacrificial fires rising from the temples. The shops that sold animals for sacrifice closed due to lack of business. No one burned incense at the small heathen altars throughout the main square. Even so, a few Ninevites who had hardened hearts like Muska refused to call on the true God, stubbornly waiting for the not-so-great gods of Assyria to come through.

There was wailing among the families of the city. But this time it was not because children were taken from them. They wailed because of thirst and hunger from fasting, and the fearful expectation that their great city and home may be destroyed soon.

Several days later a messenger reports to Nabukinuzur. "Governor, it looks like nearly the entire city is calling on God in obedience to the decree. I estimate over one hundred thousand of our fellow Ninevites are calling on God and fasting. However, there remain some holdouts here and there. Should we have them arrested for disobeying the king's decree?"

"No," said Nabukinuzur. "We must trust that just like God was willing to spare the infamous cities of Sodom and Gomorrah for the sake of ten righteous people, he is also willing to spare Nineveh, and maybe even all of Assyria, for the sake of the one hundred thousand who are lifting their prayers to him."

"Governor, when will we know if that is so?" asked the messenger. "The people ask me, but I know not what to tell them."

Nabukinuzur said, "If our understanding of the ancient Hebrew writings is accurate, we will know at sunrise tomorrow. That is the seventh anniversary of the outbreak of plague in the land, which ushered in seven years of tribulation. At that moment, either Nineveh remains standing, or she will cease to be. Tell that to the people."

The messenger said, "The people will dread the coming of sunrise tomorrow. But if we are still here after sunrise, the people will bless the day."

"Better yet they bless the God who grants that day and any days thereafter," said Nabukinuzur.

𒀭 𒂍 𒀭𒌋

The Most High heard from heaven the supplication of the Ninevites. "*When God saw what they did and how they turned from their evil ways, he relented and did not bring on* [Nineveh] *the destruction he had threatened*" (Jonah 3:10).

The dreaded day arrived, and Nineveh remained standing. Some people stopped praying and fasting and began celebrating. Others cautiously continued to appeal to the Most High. A few people whose hearts were hardened, like Muska, went around saying, "See? Like we told you. Nothing happened. There was no judgment against Nineveh. Jonah's god is an impotent god of goats, camels, and slaves. Curse Jonah's god and renew your faithfulness to the great gods of Assyria."

But one fellow confronted Muska and said, "The dreaded judgment was coming, but in his grace and mercy, God canceled it. Muska, you should be ashamed for not joining in our supplication to God. I am grateful God overlooked your insolence and heard the prayers of the people instead."

Muska said, "How dare you call me insolent, you rabble? Do you not know that I am a great one?"

The fellow replied, "You *were* a great one, Muska. But now, you are just a dumb ox. I may be humble rabble, but I have the good sense to turn to the true God."

"Mind your tongue, you contemptuous man," said Muska. "You may lose it someday."

Then the fellow said, "Keep cursing the true God, and you will lose more than just your tongue, Muska. One day, you may join your overlord Malkuno in hell. But even there, you might be unwelcome."

"Stop provoking me, you worm," said Muska.

The fellow raised his right arm as if saluting Muska, and said "Hail, great one," in mockery. Those who overheard the hail had a good laugh. At that, Muska went into a rage and left.

It has been several days since the dreaded day came and went. A messenger riding a fast horse arrived at Nineveh and reported to Nabukinuzur. "Governor, I just returned from Gozan with a message from the great and honorable King Ashurdan. The violence in Gozan is over. Peace broke out. Both sides agreed to a truce. Both are negotiating in good faith. King Ashurdan offered amnesty to the rebels and agreed to hear their grievances. In turn, the rebels opened the city and received the king in peace."

"At what day did the truce begin?" asked Nabukinuzur. The messenger stated the precise day. Nabukinuzur noted it was the same as the dreaded day that Nineveh was to fall. Later that day, messengers from Ashur and Arbaha arrived and gave similar reports. "At what day did events turn around?" asked Nabukinuzur. They stated the precise day, and Nabukinuzur noted it was the same as the dreaded day that Nineveh was to fall.

The next day several messengers arrived from regions afflicted by plague. One messenger said, "Governor, something extraordinary is happening. People and animals afflicted by pestilence are recovering mysteriously. Even some thought to be already dead are showing signs of life. There are no more reports of people or animals catching disease. No longer are mountains of dead rising in the land."

"At what day did the first man or animal show signs of recovery?" asked Nabukinuzur. The messenger stated the precise day, and Nabukinuzur noted it was the same as the dreaded day that Nineveh was to fall.

Over the next several days, more messengers arrived and gave similar reports about their cities. Nabukinuzur summoned his great ones. "My esteemed great ones," he said, "reports of peace and health are coming from all over the land. The violence that afflicted our cities is over. The famine is fading. There are no more food riots. The pestilence has subsided. People and animals are recovering from disease. The farmlands are recovering. Nineveh still stands! Truly, our great national crisis is ebbing. I am very optimistic that better days are here. And know this: The long-awaited turnaround began at all those places on the precise day that Nineveh was to fall. That was the precise day that Eshai and Gabbara spoke of, based on their understanding of the ancient Hebrew writings. Can there be any doubt that the Hebrew God saved not only Nineveh, but the whole nation of Assyria? Let all give glory to the Hebrew God, healer of nations!" The great ones rejoiced at the good news.

Adorina was present as usual. She said, "Praise the God of Israel, the one true God. Give him glory and thank him for caring enough about us to send his emissary Jonah to warn us. I now understand the meaning of the vision I had when my spirit visited his throne room. He said he was coming to our land with healing in his wings, and so he did. And I praise you, Father, for your leadership during these troubled times. I am proud to be your daughter."

Nabukinuzur said, "I am proud to be your father, Adorina. I once called you a dreamer deceived by folly. I was terribly wrong."

"Governor," said Palakh, "we should hold a festival and publicly honor Jonah and his God."

"Yes, that would be appropriate," said Nabukinuzur. "I will issue a proclamation to the city. I will designate a day of worship and celebration of God. Moreover, I will issue a proclamation bestowing to Jonah honorary citizenship of Nineveh."

"What has become of Jonah?" asked Gabbara. "Does anyone know? I have not heard of him since the day before the dreaded day that Nineveh was to fall."

"Perhaps he was not sure his God canceled the judgment against Nineveh," said Eshai. "I suppose he left the city to avoid being caught up in its doom."

"What a most unusual visitor," said Gabbara. "For a thousand years, people will tell the story of that mysterious Hebrew who came to our land and left his mark on our destiny, who then disappeared as mysteriously as he first appeared. Perhaps one day, the Hebrew scribes will record the story of Jonah in their own sacred chronicles."

"And it will be more than a fish story," said Adorina.

"A fish story?" asked one of the great ones, with a puzzled look on his face. "What do you mean?" Nabukinuzur, Palakh, Eshai, Gabbara, and Elqosh knew exactly what Adorina meant. They laughed while most of the great ones appeared dumbfounded.

"Great ones, if there is no more to say, you are dismissed," said Nabukinuzur.

"Father, will we ever see Jonah again?" asked Adorina.

"I do not know, daughter," replied Nabukinuzur. "I suspect God has more adventures planned for his servant Jonah. But this I know: Wherever Jonah goes, God will be with him, always."

"Father, will this time of peace last?" asked Adorina. "Or will the people fall back into their old ways and forfeit the blessings of God that are upon us now?"

"I do not know, daughter," replied Nabukinuzur. "But for now, let us savor the moment. Come, we have a wedding to plan."

𒀭 𒂍 𒀭𒌋

And so, the great city of Nineveh and the nation of Assyria were given a new lease on life. As went Nineveh, so went Assyria. The land was free of plagues, bad omens, wars, and rumors of war. Assyria's neighbors also enjoyed peace, for they were no longer subjected to wars of conquest.

Ashurdan returned to Nimrud after successfully negotiating peace with the rebels of Gozan. Usually, when an Assyrian king returns from a campaign, he has a triumphal procession. Two chariots would lead the procession, carrying the standards of the great gods, followed by a parade of Assyrian soldiers, long rows of prisoners escorted by soldiers, wagons filled with spoils of war, a parade of musicians and entertainers, and finally, the king riding his chariot, pulled by war stallions. The procession would stop at a temple of the great gods for the king to offer homage, and then proceed to the king's palace. Crowds would be cheering the king's triumphant return. But Ashurdan's return was different. His chariot was pulled by donkeys instead of war stallions. There were no parading soldiers, prisoners, wagons, musicians, or entertainers. Only a small squad of soldiers accompanied Ashurdan as he entered the citadel. There were no cheering crowds. Ashurdan headed directly to the northwest palace. He did not bother to visit a temple of the great gods. His return to Nimrud was the quietest kingly return in memory.

Ashurdan settled into his throne room. He ordered his aides to give him the latest news. They gave him encouraging reports about conditions throughout the land. They told him that pestilence is fading, farmlands are producing food, and there is peace in the cities. Ashurdan rejoiced upon hearing that Assyria's seven-year tribulation is over. He summoned his royal scribe and said to him, "Let it be recorded for all time in the chronicles of the kings of Assyria that in this year of Bel-Taggil, there is peace in the land. Moreover, let it be recorded for all time in my royal inscriptions that in this year of Bel-Taggil, Assyria received an emissary of the Hebrew God. The emissary declared the word of his God, and the word set us on the path to peace. Let the people of the land give glory to the Hebrew God."

𒐊 𒂊𒊺 𒐊𒌋

Not every Ninevite was happy with the outcome of Jonah's visit. Muska was already conniving with disenfranchised heathen priests to bring back the gods of Assyria. "We will rise again," said Muska at a gathering of the priests. "In a little while, the people will forget what happened here. They will say the story of Jonah is just a myth. They will clamor for the return of the great gods."

A royal scribe who attended the gathering was asked how the events will be recorded in the chronicles of the kings of Assyria. He said, "We will just write the words 'peace in the land,' without explanation. We will give no glory to the god of goats, camels, and slaves."

"But what if the king chooses to mention Jonah or Jonah's god in his royal inscriptions?" asked a priest.

The royal scribe replied, "After the king goes to be with the gods, we will smash any tablets that mention Jonah or his god. We did this sort of thing before, when we smashed many of the tablets of King Adadnirari, who told the people to worship only one god. Unfortunately, Bel-Tarsi-Iluma, that foolish governor of Nimrud in those days, had Adadnirari's decree inscribed on statues of the great god Nabu. No one dared smash those statues and so desecrate the idols. Were it not for the folly of Bel-Tarsi-Iluma, no one would remember Adadnirari's ludicrous dabbling in worship of only one god to the exclusion of the rest."

Someone else was not happy about the repentance of the Ninevites: Jonah was very displeased and angry.

He prayed to the LORD, "Isn't this what I said, LORD, when I was still at home? That is what I tried to forestall by fleeing to Tarshish. I knew that you are a gracious and compassionate God, slow to anger and

abounding in love, a God who relents from sending
calamity. Now, LORD, take away my life, for it is better
for me to die than to live.

—Jonah 4:2–3

𒈾 𒂗 𒈾𒌋

One day, Rabbu noticed Tamraz walking about the square with a woman, a boy, and a girl. "Tamraz, who are your friends?" asked Rabbu.

"Rabbu, meet my bride-to-be Emmita, her son Garsa and her daughter Lawita," said Tamraz. "As you can see, I finally settled for one woman. We will become an instant family."

"My heartiest congratulations," said Rabbu. "Adorina and I will be honored to host your marriage ceremony at our house."

"Thank you, Rabbu," said Tamraz. "I will be happy there. I certainly prefer to be married at a friend's house. I do not like the thought of marrying in a temple of our not-so-great gods."

"I also thank you, Rabbu," said Emmita. "You are most generous."

"Emmita, do your shopping with the children," said Tamraz. "I need to speak with Rabbu for a moment."

"Yes, Tamraz," said Emmita. "I will not be long. Farewell, Rabbu."

"Tell me, Tamraz, how did you come to know Emmita and her children?" asked Rabbu.

"I knew her husband well," said Tamraz. "He was killed by Malkuno's mob. Since then, I have become attached to Emmita and her children. I am quite fond of the three. She is a widow who needs a husband. Her two children need a father, and I need one woman to settle down with. We are right for each other."

"You will have a lot of responsibility," said Rabbu. "You will have to learn to be a husband and a father at the same time."

"Yes," said Tamraz. "I must set a good example for the children. There will be no more hanging out in taverns for me and no more brawling in the streets. The strong dog is tamed. I must admit, it is challenging."

A moment later, Emmita and the children returned with some wares. Garsa was holding a spear.

"Tamraz, will you show me how to throw a spear?" asked Garsa.

"I will, young man," replied Tamraz. "You will grow up to be lion brave."

Later that day, Rabbu played the Royal Game of Ur with his wife, Adorina. They enjoyed a delicious platter of fresh locust and tasty dipping sauce with cups of wine. After some conversation with Rabbu, Adorina looked at the game board and noticed that Rabbu's game pieces had outmaneuvered her game pieces. Rabbu finally beat Adorina at the Royal Game of Ur. That was a day like no other for Rabbu.

THE END